For Mary TallMountain

1918–1994

RUNNING
WILD

RUNNING
WILD

LUCY JANE BLEDSOE

MARGARET FERGUSON BOOKS
HOLIDAY HOUSE · NEW YORK

The publisher wishes to thank Sam Alexander, Gwichyaa Gwich'in from Fort Yukon, for his expert review of the text.

Margaret Ferguson Books
Copyright © 2019 by Lucy Jane Bledsoe

Printed and bound in September 2019 at Maple Press, York, PA, USA
www.holidayhouse.com
First Edition
1 3 5 7 9 10 8 6 4 2

Library of Congress Cataloging-in-Publication Data

Names: Bledsoe, Lucy Jane, author.
Title: Running wild / Lucy Jane Bledsoe.
Description: First edition. | New York : Margaret Ferguson Books ; Holiday
    House, [2019] | Summary: "When living in the Alaskan wilderness with her
    survivalist father becomes intolerable, 12-year-old Willa sets out on a
    journey of escape with her younger brothers"—Provided by publisher.
Identifiers: LCCN 2019000891 | ISBN 9780823443635 (hardback)
Subjects: | CYAC: Survival—Fiction. | Fathers and daughters—Fiction.
    Runaways—Fiction. | Brothers and sisters—Fiction. | Single-parent
    families—Fiction. | Family life—Alaska—Fiction. | Alaska—Fiction.
    BISAC: JUVENILE FICTION / Action & Adventure / Survival Stories.
    JUVENILE FICTION / Family / Siblings. | JUVENILE FICTION / Girls &
    Women.
Classification: LCC PZ7.B6168 Run 2019 | DDC [Fic]—dc23
LC record available at https://lccn.loc.gov/2019000891

RUNNING
WILD

ONE

WHEN THE SUN starts to rise, a dim light leaks through our cabin window, revealing the contents of our lives: four cots with sleeping bags, the black cast-iron woodstove with its pipe shooting up through the roof, a rough-hewn wooden table and four chairs, our cooking pots hanging from the wall opposite my bed. It's early October, and in a few weeks, the sun won't rise at all.

I am twelve years old and live with my dad and ten-year-old twin brothers, Keith and Seth, in the heart of the Alaskan wilderness. We moved here five years ago after Mama died. At first, the hard work, the bright Arctic summer sun, even the intensity of the dark northern winter, seemed to scour away our sadness. Dad's dream of living off the land, by our own wits and labor, was so forceful it carried us along like a swift current. As much as we missed Mama, we laughed a lot in those early years and Dad tried to make it fun, teaching us how to identify edible plants, helping us build a raft for messing around on our stream, and showing us how to play chess. But over the years life here has gotten harder, not easier, and so has Dad. If we complain, he says, "Humans are animals, nothing more. We need to eat, drink, sleep, that's it. Just like the bears and crows. The sooner people realize they're nothing special, the better off we'll be as a species."

I get up and reach deep into my sleeping bag to fetch my notebook. Keeping a journal was Dad's idea. He called me the family scribe and wanted me to document everything. How the helicopter dropped us off with just the basics, including some food to get us started, a big tent, the parts for our woodstove, a few tools, pots and utensils, packets of seeds, and the encyclopedia set. How over the course of that first summer we built our cabin and planted our garden, hunted for game, fished for trout and salmon, and dried and stored food for the winter. How Dad made our table, chairs, and rowboat from scratch.

Sometimes when I read these earlier journal entries, I laugh at my big blocky childish printing, with all the corrections and additions in Dad's handwriting. He hasn't asked to see my journal in over a year, but even so, I keep it hidden because he wouldn't like reading what I've been writing about lately—the things I want and miss—and that I'm worried we're not going to survive this winter.

Dad and the boys have been hunting almost daily this autumn, hiking for miles through the wilderness, searching for moose and deer. With zero luck. Most nights they fall into bed right after dinner and sleep hard. Now Dad is snoring loudly and the twins, so thin they barely mound their sleeping bags, their little-boy eyelashes fluttering with dreams, are deep in sleep. I yank jeans over my long underwear and put on my parka, grab my boots, and slip out the door.

I forgot socks, but shove my feet into the boots anyway, tie the laces tight, and pull my fleece hat and gloves from my parka pockets. I walk down to the creek, the musical ripple running through our lives. Dad made up its name: Sweet Creek.

Our rowboat sits on the small pebbled beach. About a hundred yards downstream, the creek bends out of sight. Eventually it flows into a bigger stream that runs into the powerful Yukon River, which leads to Fort Yukon, a town just a short distance from the Arctic Circle. I've only been to the settlement once, when we first came to Alaska. Dad makes this journey once a year, in the early summer, after the big melt. He brings back things like beans, rice, peanuts, cornmeal, oatmeal, bullets, matches, first-aid supplies, new boots and clothes. Opening those packages is always so exciting. Sometimes he tucks a few oranges, or a hunk of cheese, in with our staples, treats that last about three minutes. Dad doesn't like indulgences, but we all love chocolate, and he never fails to buy bags of chocolate chips so I can make cookies. This year I was shocked to see that he also brought back whiskey bottles—Dad's a recovering alcoholic and had been sober for seven years before Mama died. She always said how proud she was of him for stopping drinking.

Dad can do the round-trip journey to Fort Yukon in less than a week. While he was away, he used to leave us with Clarissa and Robert Slone-Taylor, who live fifteen miles up Sweet Creek in their own log cabin. It's my favorite week every year. We play board games, learn new songs, and even perform plays that we make up. The Slone-Taylors have more luxuries than we do, including lots of drawing paper and colored pencils. Seth spends most of the time drawing. Keith likes to help them tinker with the generator, which makes power for their cabin.

But last summer Dad had an argument with the

Slone-Taylors. As we were leaving, Clarissa said that it wasn't any of her business, and she knew everyone in Alaska carried firearms, but she and Robert both thought the twins were too young for rifles. Dad launched into a tirade, saying that every child as young as five years old in Fort Yukon has his or her own rifle. Besides, Dad carried on, no one tells him how to raise his own children. Consequently, we didn't get to go to the Slone-Taylors' cabin this summer.

"You're twelve and ten, after all," Dad said. "Bear cubs leave their mothers and start living on their own at the age of two."

He left for Fort Yukon in late June, and he was right. My brothers and I did just fine, even though he stayed away for two weeks this trip. When he wasn't home on time, I acted as though I'd known all along that he would be gone longer than usual and I told the boys that he had lots of business in Fort Yukon. Of course they asked what business, so I made up answers, like "banking" and "phoning relatives," and then had to explain what banking is and who our relatives were. Truly, after the eighth day of his absence, I wondered if he'd ever return and worried that he'd had an accident somewhere along the route. I have never been so relieved as I was when he came rowing up our creek in early July.

This morning I turn my back on the creek and face our small collection of buildings. We are surrounded by forest, but the cabin sits on a level spread of meadow between the creek and the hill where the helicopter dropped us off. There are also three outbuildings near the cabin: the woodshed; the cache, a tiny house with an airtight door on tall stilts with a ladder running up the front, where we store our food to keep it away from animals; and the outhouse. Dad carved a moon on its door, back when he still took time for fun details.

On my way to the outhouse, I walk past the woodshed. Usually by this time of year we have a big stack of firewood. We do gather wood in the winter, too, but even so, we fell short last year during the coldest month of January, when we couldn't get out much, and had to ration our fires, going to bed early to keep warm. Dad even burned our encyclopedia set. He did the first volume in a fit of frustration, because the kindling was wet, but when he saw how upset I was it seemed to spur him on, as if my wanting to read all those articles was a weakness. He said the laws of biology were the only knowledge we needed. Every day after that, he burned another volume. I used to love studying the maps, reading about astronauts and stars, finding pictures of Chinese, Namibian, or Guatemalan girls and pretending they were my friends. When I asked Dad about our fire-wood supply the other day, he waved me off, saying he couldn't take any time away from hunting.

After quickly using the outhouse—inside there is a hole cut in a wooden bench suspended over a deep earthen pit—and rinsing my hands in the creek, I climb the hill, kicking through the mat of yellow and brown leaves. At the top, the first rays of sun are spiking above the evergreen horizon. I love that moment when the sunlight first touches me.

I sit in the crunchy leaves and start writing. The boys are too young to remember much about our life with Mama in Seattle, but I'm not. I write about how I miss Pike Place Market in Seattle, where you can buy every kind of fruit and vegetable, where musicians serenade the shoppers, where we used to stop and chat with neighbors. I miss school and looking things up on a computer. I miss sleepovers and birthday parties. The smell of libraries, all those books that have been held by dozens of hands. And Christmas lights, the way Seattle gets twinkly for the holidays. I miss having my own bedroom.

I miss Mama.

I also write about Dad standing right here, on top of the hill, yesterday at dusk, shooting his rifle into the air, shouting at the sky. When I called out that supper was ready, he just looked at me and headed into the woods. He didn't come back to the cabin until well after dark and then he poured himself a tin cup of whiskey, ignoring the plate of beans and cornbread I'd left out for him.

When I'm done writing, I stuff the journal into the front of my parka and head down the hill to the cabin. Dad is stoking the fire in the woodstove, and he turns to scowl at me. He has black hair, which he cuts himself without using a mirror, so it stands out in tufts all over his head. He has a long black beard that he never trims. He's skinny. We all are. But his skinniness is winnowed and ropy; any meat left on his frame is muscle. His hands are scarred and chapped. His eyes are a startling glacier blue.

"Where have you been, Willa?" he asks.

"The outhouse."

"You've been gone a long time."

"I took a walk."

Seth and Keith are awake, watching from their cots as I take off my parka and sneak the journal under my sleeping bag.

In one stride Dad's at my side pulling the journal out. "Why are you hiding this?"

When I don't answer he brandishes it in the air over his head. "I asked you a question."

"Willa's the family scribe!" Seth calls, maybe hoping to distract him.

"I asked why you're hiding this," he repeats.

"You won't like what I've been writing."

"What have I told you about keeping secrets?"

"I'm not keeping secrets."

"Secrets are the same as lies," he says. "And I can't abide lies."

"I haven't lied—I've only written the truth."

The boys sit still, waiting to see what will happen next.

"You're twelve years old. What do you know about truth?"

His clear blue eyes, bright with a million ideas, used to reassure me; now their coldness scares me. And yet I can't keep quiet. "I know a lot."

Dad huffs in anger, two ragged expulsions of breath.

"Give it back to her," Keith says.

Dad glares at him, at me, and back at him.

"It's hers," Keith yells.

"Never mind," I whisper, knowing I can't keep Dad from reading it.

He stares at us, as if his children have grown into creatures he doesn't understand, then takes my journal out to the front porch, where he begins to read. Though it's cold out, he doesn't put on his parka. Dad likes to brag that nothing can kill him. Getting hit by a large branch when he was felling trees to build our cabin didn't. Accidentally eating a poisonous mushroom didn't. Falling through the ice into the creek two winters ago didn't. He thinks the Alaskan air only toughens him.

"It's okay," I tell the boys. "It'll be fine."

But I can't help worrying what Dad will think when he reads how scared I was that Seth might have gotten gangrene and died the time he sliced his toe with the ax. How Dad forgot all of our birthdays this year. How angry he gets when Keith talks back. How impatient he is with Seth's dreaminess. How distraught he looked shooting his rifle up into the sky at nothing at all on the hill yesterday. How his grand survival experiment is failing.

I make Seth and Keith bowls of oatmeal. Soon after they finish, Dad returns and goes straight to the woodstove. He tears out a handful of pages from my journal and shoves them into the fire. He tears out another handful and then another. All my dreams, hopes, stories, and fears are devoured by the flames. The journal is gone.

TWO

"**BOYS, GET DRESSED.** Willa, pack our lunch."

Dad taught me to shoot, and I used to hunt with him while the boys tagged along. But when he decided they were old enough to use rifles, I started staying behind because it made sense for one of us to take care of chores. I've taught the boys to cook, and they help me when they're around, but for the most part, food preparation has become my job.

As soon as they leave, I open the front of the woodstove. The ashes look like a pile of black leaves. A corner of the notebook is unburned but there is no point in pulling that out. I toss in a couple more pieces of wood to feed the blaze before closing the stove door.

It's a beautiful fall day, the sky a searing blue.

Refusing to cry about my journal, I put my hand over the left side of my chest, where my skin is puffing out into a whole new shape, and count a hundred heartbeats. Then I get to work, sweeping the floor with our homemade broom, hauling water up from the creek, and setting the metal pail on top of the woodstove to heat for washing the breakfast dishes. I clean the outhouse, using another pail of water, evergreen branches for scrubbing, and soap made from rendered animal fat.

By now, the stovetop water is hot enough for the breakfast dishes. Once they are dried and put away, I head outside and climb the ladder to our cache to take an accounting of the remaining food. Pride keeps Dad from buying many staples on his annual trips to Fort Yukon. He still believes we can catch, kill, and harvest most of our food. But we fell dangerously short last year, and in June I told him he needed to get more food in town. He laughed and said we'd be fine. My garden did well at the beginning of summer; the lettuces formed giant heads, the kale sprouted colossal green leaves, and the zucchinis grew long and fat. Because of the constant daylight during the summer up here in the Arctic, vegetables grow really big. But those are foods we eat as soon as we pick them. Without a freezer, or the means to preserve the food we grow, not much of our garden produce can be stored for the winter. This year the pumpkins and butternut squashes, which can be cached for months, got attacked by pests. The ones that did grow are small. Even the potatoes are only the size of big marbles. I check what's left of the dried meat. There's so little: the boys must be sneaking snacks.

I take a piece of venison and return to the cabin, where I put it in a pot of water to soften up for our evening stew. There's some leftover cornbread, and it would taste good with jelly, so I walk to the rose hips patch to pick the last of this year's fruit. After scooping out the seeds, I cook them on the woodstove with cinnamon and sugar. They're a great source of vitamin C, and they taste good, too. I've already made a bunch of rose hips fruit leather that we can eat all year long.

Once my chores are done, I fetch *Jane Eyre* out from under my cot. Dad had tossed it to me when we were still in Seattle, packing to come up here. He said, "Take this." Since then I've read the novel cover to cover so many times I practically have it memorized. How lonely Jane was after her best friend, Helen, died. How I wish I could take Helen's place and be Jane's best friend. When Dad began burning the encyclopedia, I hid *Jane Eyre* and now only read it when he's gone.

I curl up on my cot and start reading at the beginning,

not stopping until the cold gets me up. The fire in the woodstove has burned down to coals. After adding some wood, I look out the window and see that the sky has pearled up, become glossy and opaque. A few snowflakes drift down. I shiver. Soon freeze-up will arrive, turning the streams and even the bigger rivers into solid blocks of ice. This happens quite suddenly, usually around the middle of October. Already, on some mornings, a lace of ice trims the shore of our creek.

I dread the coming winter. In Alaska, the season is bone-rattling cold. We spend hours shoveling paths connecting our buildings. The worst part is the darkness. For most of November through January, there is *only* night. We live so far north that the sun barely rises during the winter months, and when it does, at the beginning and end of winter, it's only for a short time. I hate the darkness and how we're mostly stuck inside for the long months, hibernating like bears.

Dad and the boys should be back soon. It's time to put the venison, with some potatoes, on top of the woodstove. An hour later, at the beginning of dusk, the snow is falling steadily and they still haven't returned. What if they don't ever?

Going out onto the porch, all I can see are dark swaying trees and falling snow.

But wait. I hear something. A moment later, spots of brightness bob through the trees—the light of three headlamps.

Dad is laughing! They must have gotten game.

When they appear in the clearing, they look like snowmen, white from head to toe, and the boys are stumbling with exhaustion. Dad drags a thick tarp that he's using as a makeshift sled to bring back the meat. Their backpacks, too, will be loaded with the kill, packed into large plastic garbage bags. The light from their headlamps spills out onto the snow, making it blue and shiny.

I wait on the porch, excited to see what they've got. Dad would have skinned, gutted, and quartered the animal in the field. Unless it was something small, they would have had to leave a lot of it out there because they couldn't possibly carry that much meat. Wolves will quickly eat what they left.

"Moose," Keith says, the extreme fatigue making his voice hoarse.

"Moose!" I cry. My mouth waters at the thought.

The boys drop their rifles and packs on the porch. Inside, they tear off their parkas and pry off their boots, leaving everything in a wet heap. As Dad hauls the meat inside, I ladle bowls of the venison stew and set out the cornbread and rose hips jelly. The boys inhale their supper before crawling into their sleeping bags and falling asleep.

Dad changes into his other pants and makes himself a cup of coffee. He sits in front of the woodstove, almost smiling, and I wonder if he's forgotten what he read in my journal this morning. I pull one of the chairs over next to him and put his supper on it. He nods his thanks and wolfs it down.

I clean and dry off the firearms and return them to the high cupboard, hang the boys' wet parkas on hooks by the door, and set their boots near the stove to dry. I take a moment to pull their sleeping bags up around their shoulders and kiss each of their foreheads before gathering up Dad's Carhartts, soaked with blood from the field butchering, and putting them in the washing tub. They'll need to be cleaned with cold water because hot water cooks blood into fabric. Tomorrow I can scrub them with rocks and water from the creek.

The meat has to be preserved right away to prevent contamination. In the daylight, and in decent weather, we can work outside. But I know Dad doesn't want to wait until tomorrow. We can't risk losing any of this meat. He spreads two thick pieces of plastic on top of the kitchen table and we get to work.

First he slices off the fat for me to render. I put it into a pot on top of the stove and begin melting it down. Dad cuts the meat into smaller pieces and we apply salt cure to all the surfaces; this will help kill dangerous micro-organisms. We'll hang the salted meat chunks from the ceiling of the cache for a few weeks. Later we'll set up the big tent we lived in when we first got here, which we now use to cold-smoke meat over a slow-burning fire. Dad fashioned a hole in the tent that a chimney fits through and built a wooden rack to hold the meat at the exact right height over the fire.

We don't finish until dawn, when it's time for me to make breakfast. The boys wake up and I give them big bowls of oatmeal, dolloped with the rest of the jelly. I also roast a hunk of the fresh meat and cut chunks for them. The mood in our cabin is the cheeriest it's been in months. As everyone scarfs down their breakfasts, Dad lets the boys tell the hunt story. How Keith is the one who first spotted the moose. How Dad killed him with one shot. How lucky we are to have the slippery surface of snow because that meant they could trans-port more of the meat home than if they'd had to carry it only in their packs. Everyone is still hungry, so I mix up some biscuits and as they bake, we tell stories from past adventures. It feels almost like it did in the beginning, when we first moved up here and were all so sad about Mama, and yet had hope that this life would heal us.

Only now, as we're eating the biscuits, do I notice that I left *Jane Eyre* on top of my sleeping bag. Getting the moose has put Dad in a good frame of mind, but I don't want to take any chances. When he's not looking, I shove the book under my cot, into the farthest, darkest corner.

THREE

DAD SURPRISES ME by not even bothering to travel back to the site of the kill to see if any edible parts of the moose remain. It's not like him to admit defeat, even to wolves. But he's been up for well over twenty-four hours and looks exhausted. When he finally goes to bed, the boys get back in their sleeping bags for another snooze. I'm exhausted, too, but I want to start soaking Dad's Carhartts. I grab the washing tub and bucket and slip out of the cabin. Several inches of snow cover the ground, and the sky is a delicate pink without a cloud in sight.

After using the bucket to fill the tub and sloshing the pants a few times, I leave them on the bank while I climb the hill to feel the sun. Near the top, I hear something whimper. I walk toward the sound, suspicious of what I'll find.

Two weeks ago, a lone wolf came into our clearing. She squinted at me and then pointed her nose at the sky and howled before running off. She returned the next day, when Dad was fixing a leak in the rowboat. He shouted and clapped his hands to scare her away.

But in the morning, we saw her tracks circling the cabin.

"What does she want?" Seth asked, his voice full of wonder.

"Something tender to eat," Dad answered angrily. "Something easy to catch."

Seth is like Mama, gentle but resolute. He even looks like her with his dark-blond wispy hair, his extra-pink lips, his pale skin with the veins showing blue at his temples. He said, "We could give her something. If she's hungry."

"Your portion?" Dad asked.

"Besides," Keith said, "feed her and she'll come back for more. She'll bring the rest of her pack."

"She's a loner," Dad said. "Otherwise she'd be with her pack now."

Keith winced, not liking to be contradicted. He has eyes like Dad's, lit from within, but gray rather than bright blue. His wavy mink-brown hair hangs well below his ears because he hasn't let me cut it this fall.

The next day the wolf came back an hour before dusk. The light was thick and golden like honey, but the air was frigid. It was one of the first cold days of the season, and the boys and I were searching for round stones to use in our beds. We like to set them on top of the woodstove during supper. After they get nice and hot, we wrap them in our flannel shirts and put them in the bottom of our sleeping bags to keep our feet warm.

We didn't see the wolf walking up the stream toward us until she was close. Even after we spied her, none of us moved. I could tell Seth thought she was beautiful by his quick intake of breath.

Wolves don't eat people. They like hoofed mammals, like deer, moose, and caribou, as well as snowshoe hares and beavers. Still, it was curious that this wolf had been so bold, coming around our cabin. They usually avoid people. For a long moment, I held her gaze, feeling a mix of awe and fear. She *was* beautiful, and yet with one lunge she could rip us to shreds.

"Don't move." Dad's voice, low but forceful, came from the front porch, where he raised his rifle.

"No!" Seth cried.

I pulled my brothers into a tight hug. Keith's thin

chest trembled and a short hard sob heaved out of Seth's mouth, a hideous sound, as if he was going to throw up.

Dad shot the wolf.

Seth squirmed away and took off running up the hill.

"I hate you," Keith yelled, but Dad had already gone back inside. Keith gathered a handful of rocks and chucked them, as hard as he could, against the side of our cabin.

"We need to bury the wolf," I said to make him stop. We dug a grave in the woods and dragged the body over. I kept hoping Dad would come out to help us, but he didn't. Once we finished, we crouched next to the stream in the dark, and washed off.

I made polenta with pumpkin for dinner that night. Seth sat on his cot, tears streaming down his face, and refused to eat. Keith ate with Dad and me at the table, but in big gulping bites. Then he stood by the woodstove, as far from Dad as he could get, glowering.

"There was no other way, children," Dad said. "Either we kill her or she kills us. That's why we're up here: to live in the heart of the truth."

"Wolves don't kill people," I said.

"Game is scarce this year. She was getting too comfortable with us."

Keith used two pieces of kindling to drum on the stovetop.

"Stop that," Dad said.

Keith drummed louder.

Dad stood up from the table, took a step toward Keith, and that's when Seth cried out, "I miss Mama!"

We all froze. We never talk about Mama.

Dad sat back down, and Keith stopped drumming.

Now, as I walk toward the sound of whimpering, it becomes all too clear why Seth ran up the hill after Dad shot the wolf. He knew the wolf was someone's mother.

I find the den on a steep part of the hillside. The mother wolf had dug it out under a fallen log. It appears that, since her death, Seth has taken it upon himself to protect the lone pup. He's fashioned a door across the opening by weaving together willow branches and securing the ends with big stones. A little black nose pokes out from between the branches, and the pup begins yipping. He thinks his next meal is about to be served.

This explains the recent depletion of our meat stores. I'm guessing the pup didn't get fed yesterday, due to the long hunt, which is why he's whining this morning. I'm just glad it's me who's discovered him, and not Dad.

Standing in the thick mat of snow-covered autumn leaves, with my back to the den and the pup, I look out toward the mountains in the distance. I know it will break Seth's heart if I free the pup. But even if we could keep him hidden from Dad, we can't give him any more meat. Besides, any day now the pup will be strong enough to tear apart Seth's willow-branch gate. I pull it away and jump back. But the wolf pup just sits on his haunches and looks up at me. He licks his little muzzle and whimpers.

"Go on now," I whisper. "*Go.* You're free."

FOUR

"I WISH," KEITH SAYS at dinner, "that we could
have brought back the moose's antlers. They were *huge*."
He demonstrates by curving his arms up over his head.
The light from our table candle flickers across his face,
brightening his excitement.

"You can't eat antlers," Dad says, pushing his empty
plate away and filling his tin cup with whiskey.

"For the cabin," Keith says. "Like over the door." He
starts telling the story of the hunt all over again, elabo-
rating on the moment when he first spied the moose.

Dad interrupts him. "Since when have you become
such a chatterbox?"

Keith's face darkens. "I'm not a chatterbox."

I reach across the table and touch his arm.

Meanwhile, Seth is sulking. I figure he's been to the wolf den and found the gate torn away. He can't say anything, though, because he knows he shouldn't have been trying to keep a wild animal.

"Anyway," Keith says, "you're the one who made too much noise by tripping over a branch and scaring away the first moose we saw."

Until now, none of them had mentioned a first moose.

"Keith," I warn.

I don't remember Dad when he was a drinker. He quit when I was born. In fact, Mama once told me that he quit *because* of me. Having a child and wanting to be a good father made him see that he had a problem. Since he brought the bottles back from Fort Yukon this July, he's mostly left them alone. Days go by and he doesn't take a drink. But when he does pour himself one, he keeps drinking until he falls asleep.

"We wouldn't be eating fresh moose steak right now," Keith carries on, the heat rising in his voice, "if I hadn't found another one."

"Quiet," Dad says.

Keith forks the rest of his meat into his mouth. Seth isn't eating, so I cover his plate and put it aside for later. I use my eyes to direct my brothers over to their cots.

They mind me. But Seth starts humming a song to comfort himself.

"Seth," I say quietly. "Not now. Please."

Dad pulls his chair up to the woodstove and sets his cup and whiskey bottle on the floor next to it. He sharpens his knife and begins whittling. He used to carve little animals for us to play with, but lately he just sharpens sticks.

We all sit in silence, listening to the slide of the knife blade along the wood.

Maybe I can reason with Dad. I make him a cup of coffee and set it next to his bottle.

"Dad?"

I wait for him to look up.

"The moose you got is great, but we still don't have enough meat for the winter."

"If we had a snowmobile and a sled like the Slone-Taylors have," Keith says, still surly, "then we could have brought *all* the meat back. We'd be set."

I shoot Keith another look to quiet him.

"Snowmobile." Dad shakes his head. He thinks that's cheating. As if trying to stay alive is a game. I can't help thinking about how, back in Seattle, Dad was a high school math teacher. Who lived his whole life in the city, until we came here. He's really smart, but we moved so fast after Mama died, and there is so much to learn about surviving in the wilderness. I feel like we've gotten this far, in part, by luck.

"We're running out of time," I say. "We don't have enough food."

Dad's cheeks sag. His lips twitch. Maybe he'll actually hear me. So I just say it. "I think we should leave."

Seth gasps. *"Leave?"*

Dad doesn't answer. He takes several more swallows from his tin cup.

I add, "Before the ice starts running and we *can't* leave."

Dad refills his cup and drinks it down in two fast gulps. "Since when do you call the shots, Willa?"

"She's right," Keith says. "We need more meat."

"I want to play chess," Seth says in a teary voice.

Dad glares at Seth, his temples pulsing, then says to Keith, "You're so worried about winter, then go chop firewood."

Keith slams out of the cabin in just his T-shirt.

"Dad!" I cry. "It's dark. And cold. We can chop wood in the morning."

I unhook my parka and Keith's, but Dad says, "Sit down."

When I move toward the door anyway, he flies out of his chair and blocks my way. "What did I just say?"

I refuse to say the words, and I hold his gaze for several seconds before I go sit on the cot next to Seth. He lets me hug him.

Dad returns to his chair, his anger filling the cabin. He doesn't pick up his knife or stick. Only the tin cup. I'm relieved to hear the sound of splitting wood coming from the woodshed. As long as Keith chops wood, he'll probably stay warm enough.

I fetch the chess set, lay the board on my cot, and stand up the pieces. "You go first." Seth's posture loosens. I make a show of studying my countermove. A couple of plays later, he takes a pawn and I groan as if it were a complete surprise to me. Seth studies my face to see if I'm humoring him. I mumble, "You're not getting any more pieces from me."

I try to keep Seth focused on the chess game, but when Dad pushes up from his chair and steps out into the dark, Seth's eyes go wide.

"It's okay," I say. "Dad's gonna bring Keith back inside. Your move."

I let him take my queen and say, "I didn't see that coming."

The wood-chopping stops. It's hard to concentrate on the game as the silence from out back lengthens. Then there's a *thud*. And another long silence.

When the door to the cabin opens, Keith steps in alone. His long hair hangs over his eyes and he's shivering hard from the cold. He shakes back his hair, revealing a swelling red patch on his jawline. I reach out and touch it, and he pulls away.

"What's that?" I ask.

"I slipped," he says, "and fell onto the chopping block."

"How come you're suddenly so clumsy?" A few weeks ago he reported falling off the cache ladder and hitting his cheek on a rock. We are a long, difficult journey away from a doctor and can't afford accidents.

Keith just shrugs. Usually when you criticize him, he argues.

Seth says, "He isn't clumsy."

"Then how do you explain all this slipping and falling?"

"He talks back."

"Shut up, Seth," Keith says, but I can tell he doesn't want his twin to shut up. He wants me to hear.

My two little brothers wait for me to say something, but I don't know what to say. I wrap Keith in his sleeping bag and have him sit next to the stove until he warms up.

FIVE

I SILENTLY CRY myself to sleep. A few hours later, a jolt of fear jerks me awake. I lift my head to see if Dad has returned. Making out a lump on his cot, I drop my head back down on the pillow and stare into the darkness.

Dad was so different when Mama was alive. He read us stories and made us his special maple-walnut pancakes. And he adored Mama. She humored him when he talked about living off the land.

"My children are going to enjoy the comfort of central heating, thank you very much," she'd say, kissing him. "I'm sorry you were born a couple of centuries too late to be a pioneer, Charles."

"It's not too late," he'd say.

"Oh, yes, it is," she assured him.

Mama's sister, my aunt Frances, flew out from New York shortly before Mama died. She told me that there were lots of ways to experience grief. I felt it like a paper bag over my head, making breathing and even seeing difficult. She said that made a lot of sense to her. Dad experienced his grief as rage. Aunt Frances said that made sense, too. But when that rage convinced him, just days after Mama died, to start making arrangements to move us to Alaska, she tried to intervene.

I listened from the door as Aunt Frances, sitting at the kitchen table, argued with Dad.

"I know Chloe would be appalled by your plans," she said.

"Chloe was perfectly cognizant of my plans."

"Chloe knew you liked to *camp*, Charles. She knew you had *fantasies* about living in the wild. But you know as well as I do that she opposed the idea. You can't take these children to live without electricity, heat, stores, schools, other people. It's...it's like you're becoming one of those whack-job survivalists."

Dad barked a harsh, cold laugh. "What does a New Yorker know about survival? What my kids need now is an honest, close-to-the-bone life."

"Charles, I understand your grief, your anger. Let's just talk this through."

"No, I don't think you do understand."

Aunt Frances sighed. "When Chloe was alive, you respected her wishes for her children. Why would you—"

"*My* children," Dad said.

"Yours and hers," Aunt Frances said quietly. Then she repeated it. "Yours and hers. She would want her children to go to school. She would want—"

"I know what my wife would want. How dare you suggest otherwise."

"But—"

Dad held up a hand to silence her. "Too late. I've bought the land. It's done. We're going. And it's exactly what my family needs. You're just the aunt. You don't have any say."

"Oh, god," Aunt Frances said, dropping her face into her hands. "I've handled this all wrong. Charles, I'm sorry."

"Handled this? It has nothing to do with you. Go back to New York and your own life. Leave us to ours."

Aunt Frances rose slowly from her chair at the kitchen table. She found me standing in the doorway and knelt down. She tried to not cry, but her voice choked up. "Sweetie, I'm so sorry about this fighting. You've lost your mother, and that should be enough to deal with." She hugged me and said, "Take care of your brothers. Remember that I love you." In a whisper, she added, "If you ever need anything, anything at all, call me."

To be honest, at that point, I sided with Dad. From what I could see, Aunt Frances just made him mad. And that definitely didn't help me, Seth, and Keith. I wanted her to leave, too. So when I found her phone number scrawled on a scrap of paper on top of my dresser, I wadded it up and threw it away. Besides, Dad said there wouldn't be phones where we were going.

A month later, a helicopter dropped us off at our homestead. We put up our tent and that very first day Dad began felling trees for our log cabin.

Now as I stare into the darkness, my eyes hot and scratchy from crying, I try to make it okay. After all, I can make soap, preserve meat, grow vegetables (some years, anyway), shoot a rifle, and build an emergency bivouac in the wilderness. Dad thinks these skills will save us.

And yet every day we get rougher and sadder and angrier.

What would Mama say if she could see Dad's bottles, how skinny we are, Keith's bruises?

I creep out of bed and light a candle. I get the roll of maps down from the high cupboard. When Dad drinks whiskey, nothing seems to wake him, but I check every few seconds just to make sure. He's snoring loudly.

Keith whispers, "What are you doing?"

"Quiet. Go back to sleep."

I study the maps, tracing the rivers with my finger. The journey to Fort Yukon in the rowboat is one long downstream float. The currents do most of the work. Sweet Creek flows into a bigger stream called Aurora Creek. That goes all the way to the Yukon River.

"Are you leaving?" Keith guesses, his voice raspy with panic.

"I can't sleep. I'm just looking."

"Willa?" Seth isn't even trying to whisper.

Dad's snoring continues without a hitch.

"Please, boys. Go to sleep."

I roll the maps back up and return them to the cupboard. I blow out the candle and slip into bed.

"Willa?" Seth says again.

Bare feet pad across the cabin floorboards. My hand catches in long shaggy hair. It's Keith crouching next to my cot. His whisper is barely audible as he asks again, "Are you leaving?"

I try to pull him into a hug, but he wiggles away.

"Answer my question," he says.

"I would never leave you."

A few huffs of breath come out of his nose, the way they do when he's trying to not cry. "Promise."

"I promise. Cross my heart."

SIX

LATELY, IF ANYONE else is up, I change my clothes inside my sleeping bag. Dad turns his back when I do this. But it's still awkward.

This morning, it's worse than awkward. Because after I've changed out of the long underwear I sleep in and into jeans, I see some blood in the crotch of the long underwear. I wad them up and slip down to the creek to rinse them. But a few minutes later, in the outhouse, I find more blood.

"Dad?" I say, bursting back in the cabin door. "Can I talk to you?"

"What now?"

I glance at my brothers. "Outside maybe?"

"You can see I'm busy packing, Willa."

I watch as he shoves things into his pack. He adds a bottle of whiskey, but a second later, returns it to the high cupboard.

"Where are you going?"

"Where do you think? Hunting."

"I'm coming," Keith says. "More manpower for carrying the meat back."

"No," Dad says, his voice rough with frustration. "I'm going farther afield this time, a couple of drainages to the north. I can travel faster alone. And making a one-man bivouac is a lot easier. I'll be gone two days, maybe three."

I fetch the first-aid kit, clunk it down loudly on the table, and take out a gauze patch, waiting for him to ask me what's wrong. But he doesn't even notice. I put the gauze patch and another fresh pair of underpants in my parka pocket.

"Good plan," I say loudly, hoping to get his attention.

He hefts his pack and, with a wave over his head, leaves the cabin. By the time I run out onto the porch, he's already hiking upstream. I start to call out to him. But I know he won't listen. He hasn't been listening for weeks.

I watch Dad disappear into the forest. Below, the icy silver stream trickles along. Above, the hard, dawn-white sky lightens. A cawing raven takes flight from a spruce tree. The realization comes in a flash.

This is our chance. The boys and I have to leave on our own. Right now.

I run to the cache and climb the ladder. I stuff some dried venison, rose hips leather, a bag of peanuts, and the last two small pumpkins into a nylon bag. I also take a big container of oatmeal. Dad always says packing light is the smartest, fastest way to travel. A big load slows you down.

I stop in the outhouse and quickly change my underwear again, this time putting the gauze patch in the crotch of the fresh pair.

Returning to the cabin, I find Seth singing a song the Slone-Taylors taught us as he sorts a pile of leaves into colors on the kitchen table.

"Where's Keith?"

Seth shrugs.

I notice that a chair has been pulled to the spot on the floor below the high cupboard. I climb up and see that two rifles are missing. I know Dad took only one.

"Why is Keith so difficult?" I cry out.

"He's not difficult," Seth says.

I guess the twins will defend each other their entire lives. Sometimes it just isn't helpful.

"I need to know where your brother has gone."

Seth pushes a hand through his sorted leaves, messing up the color-coordinated piles, and begins arranging them by size.

"Listen to me." I wait for Seth to look up. "We're leaving. We're going to Fort Yukon."

Seth's eyes go big. "When?"

"This morning. Right now."

"We don't have a cabin there."

"Pack up your sleeping bag. Get your parka, fleece hat, and mittens. Gather two tarps and also a box of matches. And plenty of rope. Pack the small pot and our tin cups, too. I'll be back soon."

"Where are you going?" he says.

"Don't leave the cabin."

Keith won't have gone upstream because that's the way Dad went. He might have gone downstream. Either that or up the hill. I decide to head up the hill since that's the more difficult route, and Keith never makes the easy choice. I find him striding through the stand of white-bark birch trees, the rifle at his side, looking for all the world like a grown man, except for his size.

"Keith!" I shout at his back.

He startles at my voice and turns fast, the rifle swinging so that it is pointed at me.

"Your rifle." I gesture at the muzzle and he lowers it. He knows to never, ever point the end of a rifle at a person, and his doing so now, accidentally, just shows how upset he is, too.

I demand, "What are you doing?"

"We need more meat."

"Dad is getting more."

"What if he doesn't?"

"We have a moose."

"We have *part* of a moose. That won't be enough."

"It'll be enough for Dad."

His eyes widen, just as Seth's had done, as he takes my meaning.

"We're taking the rowboat to Fort Yukon. Now."

He huffs, in either disbelief or excitement, I can't tell which.

I turn and head down the hill. When I get near the bottom, I look over my shoulder. Keith is still standing on the hilltop, holding the rifle, his long hair blowing in the breeze. I can't see the expression on his face, but I'm afraid it's one of resistance.

When I get back to the cabin, Seth is gone, though the things I asked him to gather are on the table. I must be out of my mind thinking I can get these two wild boys down to Fort Yukon on my own. As I stuff my sleeping bag into its sack, they come into the cabin together.

Keith puts the rifle on the table and says, "I can handle Dad."

"Sure," I say, knowing that contradicting Keith never works. "Up to now. But he's getting worse."

"I'm not afraid of him," Keith says. "I can take care of us."

The bruise on his jaw has begun to bloom into hues of blue and yellow. His straggly hair is damp with sweat.

"It's not just about that. I want friends."

"You have us," Seth says.

"I know. That's why you have to come with me."

"Dad will just come get us in Fort Yukon," Keith says. "He'll be furious."

I'm glad he's thinking about our obstacles. That means he's considering the plan. "He'll have to walk. It'll take him a long time. By the time he gets there, we'll be long gone."

"Where will we be?"

"New York."

"How will we get *there*?"

"I'll call Aunt Frances, Mama's sister."

They look at me like I'd said we're going to Mars. We might as well be. Is Aunt Frances even alive? Will I be able to find her phone number? Is she still willing to help us? If she is, how will we get to New York?

"Will we go to school?" Seth asks.

Keith huffs. "Not a good idea. Seth will get beat up."

"What are you talking about? You don't know anything about school."

"I do, too. We went to kindergarten."

"I want to stay here," Seth says. "New York is a land of robots."

"People eat unhealthy food there," Keith says.

"The air is so polluted they all have cancer."

"You're both just quoting Dad."

"I'm staying," Keith says.

I sit down on my cot, next to my pack, and make my voice soft but forceful, the way I remember Mama used to speak. "Seth, in our new life, you'll get big pads of drawing paper, your own scissors, and a set of markers in a hundred different colors. We'll get you piano lessons, too."

"Piano?" he says.

Is it possible he doesn't even remember what a piano is?

"It helps you sing," I say.

He makes a soft sound of agreement.

I turn to Keith. "Do you remember my bicycle? We can get you one."

"You're trying to bribe us."

"No, I'm not. I'm telling you about a big beautiful world out there that you deserve to see. I can remember perfectly how it felt to ride my bike really fast. It's the *best* feeling. Sometimes the kids in our neighborhood would race."

That last word gets Keith's attention.

"We'd all line up on our bikes in front of a line of chalk. We'd say, on your marks, get set, *go!* The first one to the end line would be the winner."

Keith looks away, trying to resist.

"Aunt Frances is really nice. Her face is like Mama's, only she has long, thick curly hair. She's chubbier. And she wears makeup."

Keith nods hard once, just like Dad sometimes does, and starts stuffing his sleeping bag into his pack.

"We can come back," I say. "If we don't like New York."

We divvy up the supplies on the table. I check to make sure they each have a headlamp and are wearing their rubber knee-high river boots with the thick felt lining, and not their hiking boots. We'll be on the water the whole time and with any luck, we should get to Fort Yukon in three days.

The boys cinch up their packs and run down to the rowboat. I look around, checking for anything else we might need. I take some more gauze patches from the first-aid kit, and consider taking the rifle, but I can picture Clarissa Slone-Taylor's face so clearly, telling Dad how worried she is about the boys handling a gun. It's been a long time since I've shot the rifle. We'll be in Fort Yukon soon. People don't need rifles in town, do they? I'm sure we won't need one in New York. But we will need money. I climb up to the cupboard and find the money jar, take forty-five dollars, and push the cash deep into the front pocket of my jeans. I take a new notebook and a pencil, too. Last of all, I fetch *Jane Eyre* out from under my cot and shove the book into my pack.

The boys are standing next to the rowboat tied up to the stake. Their packs sit on the ground by their feet. The gravity of what I'm about to do—take my ten-year-old brothers on an expedition in the Alaskan wilderness, on the brink of freeze-up—sinks like a rock in my belly. I step off the porch and turn to look: our cabin, our shelter, warmth, protection. Once we leave here, we have only trees and sky.

"Throw in your packs," I tell Keith and Seth. "Let's go."

"The oars," Seth says.

"Yes, them, too."

"No," Keith says. "They're gone."

I stare at the rowboat for a long time trying to make

this not be true. During the summer, Dad always leaves the oars in the boat, latched into the oarlocks, the blades resting on the bottom of the boat.

"I guess he put them away for the winter," I say.

"Seth already checked the woodshed. They're not there."

"He must have put them somewhere else."

We begin hunting for the oars. As each precious minute slides by, I get more upset. Oars don't just disappear. Dad must have hidden them. The significance of this hits me: he's anticipated the possibility of our trying to leave.

There's no point in continuing our search. Talk about looking for a needle in a haystack. Two wooden sticks in the Alaskan wilderness. He could have hidden them three miles away. Wherever they are, we're not going to find them. When Dad does a job, he does it well.

I look up at the big blue sky and want to caw like a raven. Oh, how I wish I had wings and could just take flight.

"We can walk," Keith says.

"It'd take way too long. We wouldn't have enough food."

"Let's take the raft," Seth says.

"Yes!" Keith shouts, and hugs his brother.

"I don't know." We'd made the raft by strapping logs together with heavy twine. We nailed planks, imperfect ones Dad had cast off while building the rowboat, on top of the logs. We haven't had time for playing on the raft for a couple of summers and it's stashed in some bushes out of sight. "The raft is fine for playing around on our little stream, but the Yukon is one of the most powerful rivers in the world."

"Are you kidding?" Keith says. "That raft is *tight.*"

It's a toy. And the boys never learned to swim because Sweet Creek is too shallow. Besides, after Dad discovers we're gone, he'll be able to follow us in the rowboat, which is much faster than the raft. Even with our two-day lead, he might catch us.

I stare downstream. So close. So ready. I decide it's worth the risk.

SEVEN

BY THE TIME we push off, Keith is manic with excitement. He takes the first turn with the steering pole, standing at the back of the raft and pushing the end of the long stick hard against the pebbled stream bottom. He faces downstream, his chin tipped up, as if looking into our future. The wind ruffles his long hair.

Seth and I sit on the raft with our arms around our knees. I'm surprised Seth is being so brave. His eyes are soft, that way they get when he is wide-awake dreaming, and he smiles happily.

I take a turn with the steering pole, keeping us in the center of the stream where the current is strongest, and we make good time. Everything is golden: the few remaining aspen leaves fluttering on the trees, the copper-colored stones in the streambed, and the sunlight on the water. The sun's warmth feels good, and I have a surge of hope. If we can keep this pace...If the weather stays mild...If we don't make any wrong turns...If the raft holds together...If the boys mind me...

Seth's pack squirms. It also yips.

"Seth!" I shout. "Open your pack."

"No."

"Do it."

His pale face sets into two lines, his blond brow and his tight pink lips, both straight across his face. He shakes his head.

I hand Keith the steering pole. He grins, his eyes shining.

As soon as I loosen the top of Seth's pack, a black snout pushes through the opening. The pup wiggles out and sits on a plank of the raft. He's dark silvery-gray except for white legs, a white tip on the end of his tail, and a white mask around his eyes.

He's beautiful, but he's a wolf. A wolf that Seth has smuggled on board our rickety little craft. Seth's pack is nearly empty without the pup.

"Where is your sleeping bag?"

"He'll keep me warm."

"Don't tell me you didn't bring your sleeping bag."

"It didn't fit."

"I'll share mine," Keith says.

"But how did you even catch him?" I have to ask.

"After you pulled the gate away, he ran off. I thought he was gone for good. But he wasn't. He came back and waited for me in his den."

Of course he did: Seth was feeding him.

I take the steering pole away from Keith and push us close to shore where the undergrowth is especially thick.

"He's a *wolf*," I say. "You can't keep him."

Seth wraps his arms around the pup's neck, burrowing his face in his ruff. "I've tamed him. He won't hurt us. I'm not going without Zhòh."

"You've *named* him?"

"It means 'wolf' in Gwich'in."

Fort Yukon is home to the Gwichyaa Gwich'in people. Robert Slone-Taylor has a Gwich'in dictionary that translates words into English. Seth delighted in learning some of the words back when we used to visit the Slone-Taylors.

I hate hurting him, taking away something he loves, but I pry the pup out of Seth's arms. The wolf nips my hand before I toss him toward shore. He lands in shallow water, scampers up the bank, shakes off his wet hind end, and turns to look at us.

"He'll be fine," I tell Seth, who is crying now. "He knows how to get food."

"He doesn't," Seth protests. "He's never been taught."

"He doesn't need to be taught. He's a wolf."

Keith looks sorry for his twin, but he doesn't oppose me. We watch the pup crouch down, paws stretched out on the ground in front of him, eyes pinned on our raft. Seth sobs. The wolf pup raises his nose in the air and howls. A big knot of tears snarls up in my own chest. The little wolf disappears into the brush beside the creek.

He's gone, and we're on our way again.

EIGHT

THICK UNDERGROWTH CROWDS either side of
the creek all afternoon and it isn't until the sky turns
violet with dusk that I spy a flat sandy shore backed by a
scraggly brown meadow. We beach the raft. While I drive
a stake into the sand to tie it up, I send the boys off to
collect wood. We need to get a fire going. The temperature is dropping fast, and the boys will have to share one
sleeping bag, which means they won't be able to zip it all
the way.

As I build the fire, darkness closes around our camp.
I get a good blaze going and take out the bag of peanuts.
The boys eat big handfuls—way too many if the nuts
are going to last—while I slice open one of the pumpkins
and cut the orange flesh into chunks. I poke the end of a

sharpened stick into one chunk and hold it over the fire to roast. The boys clamor for their own roasting sticks and pumpkin chunks.

"I want meat," Keith says after he finishes his portion of pumpkin.

The dried venison needs to last, but I want to keep their spirits up, so I dig into the food bag and give them each a small piece, ignoring the ache in my own belly. As they eat, I spread out one of the tarps and cover it with the two sleeping bags. I was going to ask Seth to get the other tarp out of his pack so I could rig a shelter, but it's too dark and I'm too tired. The sky is full of stars, so there probably won't be any rain or snow tonight. As the boys nestle into the one sleeping bag, I hang the food bag from a tree branch to protect it from wildlife, before snuggling into my own.

"Okay," I say, "time for your first city lesson."

"Maybe we should go back," Seth says.

"Do you remember crosswalks?" I ask, trying to sound cheerful.

Keith says, "Duh." But his voice wavers. I'm guessing he doesn't really remember.

"So people drive cars on streets," I tell them.

"I know," Keith says. "Dad says cars are bad."

"It's true that they can be dangerous because they go

really fast. So to get across the streets, there are lights. They tell you when you can go."

"Green means go! Red means stop!" Seth calls out.

"Exactly."

"We *know* this," Keith says.

"Okay. What about money? How many quarters in a dollar?"

Their silence tells me they have no idea. We spend a few minutes on quarters, dimes, nickels, and pennies. I dig the bills out of my pocket and hold them up in the firelight so they can see Andrew Jackson's picture on the twenty-dollar bill and Abraham Lincoln's face on the five-dollar bill. I make up story problems—if a book costs five dollars and twenty cents, and you give the merchant a ten-dollar bill, how much change will you get back?— and we have fun making imaginary change. Soon they fall asleep.

I can't sleep though. In the quiet of the night, I'm afraid about the blood. Every time we pulled to shore today, I hid behind a bush or tree and changed the gauze patch. I try to distract myself by listing everything I can remember about Aunt Frances. When she visited, she and Mama would sit up late, laughing hard. In the morning I'd ask what they'd been laughing about and Mama would say, "Oh, just old stories. It's like that with sisters." I told Mama that I wanted a sister, but she said our family was already the perfect size. I must have looked disappointed because she added, "Best friends are as good as sisters. When you're bigger, you'll have a best friend."

I sit up, drape the sleeping bag over my shoulders, and fish my new notebook, pencil, and headlamp out of my pack. Describing all my experiences and feelings to someone, even if that someone is just myself, always helps.

I write until a coal in the firebed pops so loudly I jump. Did something scurry at the edge of the firelight? I shine the light of my headlamp into the darkness. Nothing.

I hear a *snoof*.

Maybe I should have brought the rifle.

A blur of fur leaps into our camp. I scream for my brothers to wake up. Too late. The animal lands on top of their sleeping bag. It shoves its nose at Seth's neck.

Zhòh.

The boys yelp like pups themselves and sit up fast, knocking heads in the process. Seth shouts his joy at seeing his wolf pup. Keith smiles, too.

It takes me a few moments to recover. Then I think: something is very wrong when a wolf ambush spells relief.

"How did he get here?" I demand to know.

"He ran along the bank all day," Seth says.

"You could see him skittering in and out of the brush," Keith adds.

How did I miss that?

Seth kicks out of the sleeping bag and reaches into the front pocket of his jeans. He pulls out his share of the dried venison. I'd also missed seeing him stow that away. He feeds the meat to Zhòh.

"Don't do that!" I shout.

"Too late," Keith says.

"You can't feed a wolf."

"He just did."

Not only has Seth given some of our precious meat to a wolf, his pocket now smells of venison. He's bear bait.

The wolf pup sits behind the boys and eyes me. When I stand and clap my hands at him, he shoots back into the darkness of the tangled undergrowth.

"He'll be cold," Seth protests.

"He's a wolf," I say for about the tenth time.

"A *baby* wolf."

"Go to sleep," I say.

The boys are too tired to disobey. Seth gets back in

the sleeping bag with Keith and they curl up in the way I imagine only twins will do, and fall right back to sleep.

A few minutes later, Zhòh creeps toward the warmth of the fire, his belly dragging, as if he can keep me from seeing him if he stays low. There's no point in shooing him again. Seth has fed him meat. A wolf will risk anything for meat.

Zhòh stretches out next to my brothers, his nose on his front paws, the firelight brightening his silver coat and white-fur mask. He heaves a big sigh and closes one eye. The other eye he keeps trained on me.

In the morning I'll have to banish him again, and I'll hate doing it, I really will. Seth probably wants a friend as badly as I do. At least the boys have each other.

I think again of how Mama and Aunt Frances laughed together. What Mama said about sisters. About best friends. I try to imagine what that would be like.

I remember playing kickball on the playground, shouting and running and laughing with packs of other kids. It was so much fun. I remember Sarah, who had red hair, lots of freckles, and a loud laugh. Felicia was a quiet girl with toasty skin and serious brown eyes. She waved her hand high in the air when the teacher asked a question. Corey liked to dance. She wore deep-purple or lime-green leggings with long T-shirts. The T-shirts had messages on them, like *So Many Books, So Little Time* or *Girl Power*. If I'd stayed in Seattle, would Sarah or Felicia or Corey be my best friend?

I pick up my journal and pencil again. I can write about sitting up all night by the campfire, trying to protect my brothers. About how I wish the northern lights would come out. About how I understand why Seth loves Zhòh and yet we can't keep him. About Keith's stubborn pride. I want to describe Mama and explain Dad. All these things I can tell my journal. But it's just two pieces of cardboard sandwiching a sheaf of paper. It can't actually listen. It doesn't have its own stories.

If I had a best friend, we'd talk and talk. I'd tell her *everything*. She'd listen. Also, she'd tell *me* everything, and I'd listen.

NINE

I WAKE DEEP inside my sleeping bag, hugging my journal and watching the first dim light of the day turn the blacks to grays. Our camp is covered with a thin layer of snow. The coals of our fire are stone cold. Beyond our small meadow is a stand of Sitka spruce, the dusky needles frosted white.

"Keith! Seth!" My brothers sit side by side on a log, a good twenty yards away, their backs to me. "What are you doing?"

All my muscles are stiff and sore as I make my way over to them. They turn, their cheeks stuffed with dried meat, their jaws working it down as fast as they can. Zhòh is gnawing his own piece of venison.

"This food has to last all the way to Fort Yukon!" I

try to yank the food bag away from Keith. But he won't let go.

"We're hungry," Keith says, and keeps chewing.

Seth stands and walks across the small meadow to the crust of ice that lines the stream's edge. He gets down on all fours, uses his fist to punch through a place in the ice, and drinks as if he were a wolf himself.

Both sleeping bags are frosted. Now the knees of Seth's jeans are also wet.

The cold seeps through my parka, up under the cuffs of my pants, tingles my face. Dad could get back to the cabin by nightfall. When he finds us gone, he'll set out after us. We don't have time for a fire. Meat in their stomachs will keep the boys warmer. It'll give them energy.

"Pack up," I say. "We're leaving in five minutes."

As Seth walks back from the stream, drips of water on his chin, he stops to whistle for Zhòh.

"The wolf stays here," I say. "He's not coming with us."

I snatch the two sleeping bags and throw them on the raft, leaving them loose, hoping the sun will come out and dry them as we float, despite some splashing. As I walk back up the bank to get the tarp, Zhòh begins yipping, as if he's understood my words and wants to protest. But the pup isn't looking at us. He sits facing the forest of Sitka spruce, his behind on the ground, his front legs straight, and his nose in the air. He yips and yips.

Seth calls him again, but Zhòh launches into a run, straight toward the evergreens, barking as viciously as if he were a full-grown wolf. Back and forth, back and forth, he runs in front of the trees, growling, woofing, baying. We all stare into the darkness of the forest, trying to see what he sees or hears.

A shadow, a big shifting mass. Breath, thousand-pound huffs. She steps out from the stand of Sitka spruce, lumbers into our meadow. A brown bear.

At this close range, even with a bear's bad eyesight, she sees us. And with her excellent sense of smell, everything from the food bag Keith is still carrying to the venison on our hands—and on the inside of Seth's pocket—lets her know we're here.

Not good. But we've encountered many brown bears—called grizzlies in the Lower Forty-Eight—and I know what to do. I scan the surroundings for cubs. Brown bears are most ferocious when they have little ones. She appears to be alone.

As we start to back up, she stands. Her front legs lift off the ground and her enormous head raises to a height of at least seven feet. Her front paws hang in front of her chest. Each paw sports five claws, as long and sharp as hunting knives.

My heart pounds so hard it feels like it might beat right through the wall of my chest. Zhòh continues yipping and charging. One swipe of the bear's paw and the wolf pup would fly to his death. At least Zhòh keeps the bear distracted.

Until the bear's dim eyes pin on Keith and the food bag.

My fear turns inside out. I find, deep within myself, a deadly calm.

"Drop the food bag," I say to Keith. "Grab your packs, both of you, and back up slowly. Get on the raft. *Now.*"

Zhòh crouches his front end down to the ground, raises his behind in the air, and snarls.

"Zhòh!" Seth cries, and starts for the pup.

"Leave him."

Zhòh spins around and barks his own warning at Seth.

The bear drops down to all fours and walks toward us. Her huge head swings from side to side as her nose sniffs the air.

We're at the waterline when Zhòh makes his move. He lunges at the bear and nips her paw, then shoots away before the bear even knows what happened. It works.

The bear looks away from us and peers in the direction of the wolf pup.

It's a risk I shouldn't take, but not having food is almost as bad a threat as a bear attack. I run and make a dive for the food bag. The bear rises up on her hind feet again, towering over our camp, not twenty yards away from me. I snatch the bag before doing the thing I know I'm not supposed to do: turn my back and run. The boys, who've boarded the raft, clap their hands and shout at the tops of their voices to draw the bear's attention away from me. I yank out the stake and leap on board.

We push off with the steering pole, but the water in this stretch of the stream is lazy and we move slowly. Bears are good swimmers. If she decides we're worth the effort, she could easily overtake our raft. I dig in and push as hard as I can. Onshore, the wolf pup zips back and forth, frantic as a mosquito, yapping and yapping, doing everything in his power to distract.

"Look!" Seth shouts. "She has a cub."

Sure enough, a small brown bear splashes into the stream, coming from the bank opposite our camp. Our raft is right between the sow and the cub.

"It's so cute," Seth cries out. "Look at its soft muzzle."

The sow vaults into the stream. She displaces gallons of water, splashing so hard that drops hit my face.

Her gigantic pink tongue flops out of her mouth between two rows of huge yellow teeth. The thick muscles in her flanks ripple with the effort of moving through the water. She's so close, I can almost smell her breath.

"Seth. Keith. *Help*."

Both boys find places to put their hands on the steering pole, and we heave the raft forward. The sow stands up in the middle of the stream and roars at us. She lifts a paw and swipes at the air.

Fear makes my vision wonky, like I'm looking through a kaleidoscope, but I keep pushing, keep sinking the steering pole into the streambed and shoving with all my might.

"*Harder*," Keith yells.

Seth calls out to the bear, "We won't hurt your cub!"

I want to scream at him that bears don't speak English.

"*Heave*," Keith growls.

The raft finally swirls into a stronger midstream current. The distance between us and the two bears grows longer and longer. They wade out of the stream together and stand on the meadow where we camped, watching us float away.

"Bye!" Seth shouts.

"See what I mean?" Keith says. "He talks to bears. Just think what he'll do in New York."

The mama bear snorts, turns, and galumphs back into the spruce forest, her cub chasing behind. I leave the pole in Keith's hands and collapse on the raft, allowing myself one sob.

"Come, Zhòh! Come!" Seth calls.

"We can't—" I start to say.

"He saved our lives," Keith interrupts. "No way are we leaving him behind."

"Zhòh!" Seth calls again.

It's true: Zhòh showed fierce loyalty. I don't stop Keith from steering the raft back to shore. The wolf pup jumps aboard. Seth snuggles him, saying, "Good boy."

Keith pushes off and we waft to the center of the stream. I hold my breath, waiting for the current to sweep up under our raft and carry us away.

TEN

I TAKE THE pole away from Keith and drape the two sleeping bags over the boys' shoulders to keep them warm and to dry the bags. I fight off the deep chill in my own muscles by working hard with the steering pole.

Seth chatters away about the bears, describing everything, almost as if he were painting their pictures. It's not helpful that his feelings of awe are sometimes bigger than his feelings of fear.

Keith stands at the front of the raft, gazing north, south, east, and west, as if he's searching for something. He finally says, "Dad is going to be really mad when he catches up to us."

"He won't catch up to us." I say, faking confidence.

"The rowboat is faster," Keith points out.

"We have a big lead on him."

"I think we should go back," Keith says.

By now, midday, the sun has melted the bit of snow that fell in the night, nearly dried our sleeping bags, and thawed my tired limbs. Our raft is whipping along at a nice clip, carrying us to our future. A bald eagle soars on the wind currents overhead. Keeping my eyes pinned on the huge bird's white head, dark brown wings, and graceful flight, I pretend I didn't hear Keith.

"I'm hungry," Seth says.

"Me too," Keith says.

"That's why we're leaving," I say. "Because we don't have enough food for the winter."

"Dad is getting more meat."

"He might not find any game."

"We're big now," Keith persists. "I can hunt. I can get us *five* more moose."

"That's even enough for Zhòh too," Seth cheers.

"Yep," Keith tells his twin. "Absolutely."

I know better than to keep arguing with Keith. He's wearing his contrary face, the one where he pulls down his mouth and squints his eyes.

By dusk our muscles ache from the long hours pushing the steering pole, coupled with the return of evening's cold air. The evergreens are close on the banks of the stream here, so we camp in the woods, where there is plenty of firewood and the trees give us some shelter.

Once we've built a fire, we roast the second pumpkin and finish up the meat. From here on, it'll be oatmeal, peanuts, and rose hips leather. After dinner, the boys wrap one of the sleeping bags around their shoulders and sit next to the fire. Zhòh curls up by Seth.

We had to leave one of the tarps in last night's camp because of the bear, but we still have one left. I ask Seth to fetch it from his pack so I can rig a shelter before the boys fall asleep.

"We don't need it," he says, his voice extra-high and reedy, the way it gets when he's trying to put one past me.

"We do. Please get it."

Seth doesn't get up, the firelight dancing across his face. He's softly tugging Zhòh's ears and the wolf pup makes little grunts of pleasure.

Keith sighs, throws the sleeping bag off his shoulders, and stands. He walks over to Seth's pack, and takes out the bundle of plastic. As he unfolds the tarp in the firelight, I see that it's shredded.

Seth pulls Zhòh even closer.

Of course. Yesterday morning the puppy was closed up in the pack with the tarp. He tore it to ribbons. We have no shelter.

"I can see stars," Seth says. "It's not going to snow tonight."

"There were stars last night, too," I say, "and it clouded up and snowed later in the night."

"It doesn't matter," Keith says. "We're going home tomorrow."

Home. What does the word even mean? Keith is talking about our one-room cabin up here in the Arctic wilderness. That's not home. That's an experiment, Dad's experiment. Home was our kitchen in Seattle: the smell of simmering soup, books stacked on all the counters, Mama talking on the phone, Dad's loud laughter. Will New York be home? The encyclopedia only showed pictures of towering buildings, streets jammed with cars, brightly lit signs, and the Statue of Liberty.

What if Dad is right? What if I'm taking the boys to a life that's even more dangerous than the one we have here?

"Whichever direction," I say quietly, "backwards or forwards, we need shelter."

The boys spread out their sleeping bag and crawl in. I'm too exhausted to even gather some boughs to use as a ground cover under our beds, so I shake out my bag on the other side of the fire from the boys, get in, and fall into a deathlike sleep.

In the morning, my muscles hurt even more than they did yesterday, and my stomach clenches with hunger. At least it didn't snow again. I wiggle out of my sleeping bag. Back in the woods, I have to change the gauze bandage in my underwear yet again, burying the used one. I don't like the dull ache in my belly. I was so little when Mama died, but I will never forget her wincing with pain. What if I have the illness that killed Mama?

Returning to camp, I check for the food bag and see nothing but empty space where it should be hanging. The bag lies on the ground a few yards away, a hole chewed through the fabric, the nuts and rose hips leather gone. Even the oatmeal has been devoured. I mustn't have hung it high enough, or maybe a wolverine climbed the tree and chewed through the rope. We'll have to travel the rest of the way to Fort Yukon without food.

The boys are still asleep. I hide the ruined food bag in my pack and ready the raft. The apron of ice along the stream bank is wider and thicker than it was yesterday morning. The air is frigid. I don't know how we'll stay warm without fuel for our bodies. We'll have to do it by working harder. That way we'll get to Fort Yukon faster. Maybe we can travel at night, too, by starlight, if it stays clear.

Dad says that a body can go a long time without food,

as long as it has water. We have plenty of that. We'll be uncomfortable. But we'll live. I just can't make any more mistakes.

I wake the boys, announcing, "Let's go. We should reach Aurora Creek today."

"I told you," Keith says, not missing a beat. "We're going back."

He stuffs the sleeping bag into his pack, then hoists the load onto his shoulders and walks upstream. "Come on, Seth."

Seth says to me, "You have to come back to the cabin with us."

"I'm not going back there."

"Your choice," Keith says. He walks another few yards upstream and calls over his shoulder, "Seth! I said come on."

"She can't go to Fort Yukon by herself."

Keith keeps walking.

"You can't walk all the way back," I yell. "It'll take you *days*. Much longer than it took us to drift here on the current."

Keith doesn't stop.

Seth stands motionless between us.

"I won't spend another winter in that cabin!" I shout so loudly a couple of ravens startle off a low spruce branch.

Keith finally stops and turns. Seth's brow furrows and his lips tremble. No one says anything for a long time.

Zhòh scampers in circles, jumping in the air to snap at wind-whipped leaves.

"If we go back," I say, "Dad will shoot Zhòh."

Seth's mouth falls open and he squeaks, "No."

Keith puts his hands on his hips and looks skyward. He knows I'm right.

"I'm not going," Seth bellows.

Keith sighs, doing one of his imitations of a grown man, and starts walking back toward us. "All right," he says. "We'll take Willa to Fort Yukon. We'll make sure she gets there safely. Then we'll see."

As if he's in charge.

"Thank you," I tell Keith.

We're all surprised by the tears in my voice.

The hug is more like a tackle. Keith throws himself at my waist. His pencil arms go around me. Seth piles on. I squeeze them hard.

"He was joking," Seth tries.

It's such a ridiculous thing to say, and we all feel such relief, that we actually laugh, our gusts of breath coming out like small clouds.

"Promise you won't do that again," Seth says to Keith.

"Do what?"

"You know. Act like you're going to leave."

Keith remains silent as he steps onto the raft, and Seth yells, "Promise."

"Okay," Keith says quietly. "I promise."

Zhòh is the last to leap on. I push the steering pole through the sheet of shore ice. The current catches our raft. Once again, we're off. With any luck, we'll make Fort Yukon by late tonight.

ELEVEN

ONCE WE'RE LAUNCHED, Keith opens my pack to get at the food. He pulls out the gnawed and empty bag, fires me a look as heated as any Dad can deliver, and stuffs it back into the pack, trying to keep Seth from seeing. But Seth has seen.

"We need food," Seth whines.

"I know. We'll get some in Fort Yukon. I have money."

"When? Tonight?"

I want nothing more than to get them a hot meal. I need food, too, in order to make good decisions. My thoughts feel like watery broth. But we can survive a day without food. We just have to travel as quickly as possible.

By midmorning, it's snowing again. The snowflakes land on the surface of the stream, looking like tiny cobwebs before they melt. The ones that land on the raft stick. The ice will start running any day now and then river travel will be impossible. We have to get to Fort Yukon before that happens. I make sure the boys have on their long underwear and that their parkas are zipped to the top. I pull each of their fleece hats down over their ears. Seth doesn't mind his hearing being muffled, but Keith rolls the sides of his hat up again.

We take turns pushing with the steering pole. The work exhausts us, and yet it keeps us warm, so we all want longer turns. In the late afternoon, we come to an intersection of our stream with another one. Both streams widen with long snow-dusted gravel bars at the intersection. Big rounded indents cross these gravel bars: bear tracks. I look around quickly. The forest has given way to open country, covered by low, scraggly bushes. Thankfully, I see no brown furry mounds on any of the shores.

So I allow myself a tiny celebration. We've completed the first leg of our journey. This is our turnoff. I close my eyes and take a couple of deep breaths, mustering my hardiest voice to announce, "Aurora Creek! A few hours, at most, on this creek. It flows right into the Yukon. Then it's a short float to town."

"Tonight?" Seth asks again.

The day is October short and the sun is already low.

Plus it's snowing. Arriving tonight is unlikely. "Maybe," I hedge.

I take the steering pole from Keith and push us out of our stream and into the new one. Soon the new stream narrows considerably. It's much smaller than I thought it would be, and quite shallow. In some places, it's only a couple of feet deep. But all the waterways are at their lowest at this time of year.

It occurs to me that this is good news. Our flat-bottomed raft can skim along on the surface, but the deep-hulled rowboat will be grounded. Dad won't be able to follow us down Aurora Creek. The bright realization makes me shout, "Ha!"

"What?" Seth asks.

"We're getting there," I cheer. "Not long now."

It's snowing harder and harder. I consider not stopping to make camp for the night. We won't be able to travel by starlight, that's for sure, but navigation shouldn't be an issue. On foot, it's difficult to find your route in the dark, but rafting doesn't present many choices. We need only float down Aurora Creek until we come to the Yukon River. The convergence might have strong and swirling currents, though, and the Yukon might be too big to tackle in the dark.

Still, camping doesn't make much sense. We don't

have a tarp for shelter. We don't have any food to cook. And the falling snow will prevent us from making a fire. At least by taking turns doing the work of steering, we might stay warm.

The stream is narrowing even more. It's also becoming even more shallow. Twice already the bottom of the raft has scraped the streambed. It's one thing if Dad can't get through to the Yukon River in the rowboat, but what if we can't on the raft?

With a dark feeling of dread, I begin to wonder if this is the right creek. Even in June this current wouldn't run full enough to carry a rowboat. I try to remember the map: Were there other streams that forked off from Sweet Creek before Aurora Creek?

When the raft sticks on the muddy bottom, and this time I can't push us off, I say, "Okay, guys," in a loud confident voice, as if we're right on plan. "We're stopping for the night."

"Here?"

"Yep." The water barely comes up to our ankles in our rubber boots as we drag the raft out of the trickle of a stream. I have zero time for panic. The sky is a thick blur of snow and we need shelter.

"What's the saying about lemonade?" I ask, as if we're just playing games.

"The storm is getting worse," Keith says, refusing to play. He kicks at the snow piling up on the ground.

"When life gives you lemons, make lemonade?" Seth asks.

"Bingo. And snow means we can make a fort."

I put a hand under each of their chins and look into their eyes. "Remember what Dad taught us about making an emergency bivouac?"

I set to work rolling a snowball. Once it's a foot and a half wide, I roll another one. By now Seth has joined me. I'm thankful his imagination allows him to see the game in anything, even survival. Soon Keith starts rolling snowballs, too. Zhòh joins in, too, digging random holes in the snow, making us laugh.

A wind kicks up as we work, blowing the snow sideways. My nose runs and my eyelashes catch the snowflakes. We need to hurry. The temperature is dropping, which will make the snow drier and harder to make into snowballs. Plunging temperatures will also suck the heat from our bodies, putting us at greater risk for hypothermia.

We push the snowballs into a circle with a diameter of about five feet, leaving an opening for the door. We stack more snowballs on top of these, offset so that the growing wall leans slightly in, toward the center of the circle. The snowballs hold each other in place, and it's not long before I'm carefully setting one on the top of our fort. The boys and I pack more snow into all the spaces between the snowballs. I poke a hole in the top for ventilation. The small door will provide some fresh oxygen, too. Without a flow of oxygen, we could get carbon dioxide poisoning from our own exhaled breath.

By now I can't even feel my hands and my nose is numb, too. The wind is blowing hard, whistling its Arctic song. The trees sway and bend, promising a doozy of a storm. A nearby branch cracks as it breaks and thumps to the ground.

We squeeze through the opening of the fort, dragging our packs behind us. I place the shredded tarp on the floor. At least it'll provide a little protection. We empty our packs and place them on top of the tarp for another layer of protection from the cold snowy floor. Not the most comfy mattresses, but we need to stay as dry as possible. The sleeping bags, zipped together to make one large bag, go on top. We all slide into the single pouch, with Seth in the middle. Zhòh curls up on top of Seth's legs.

As we lie perfectly still, my brothers breathing loudly, I wriggle my fingers and toes, checking for feeling. They ache as they warm, but they do warm. Slowly, I start to realize that we're fairly snug.

Neither of the twins mentions his hunger. I don't mention that I think we've taken a wrong turn.

Seth finally says, "I might be scared."

"*Might* be?" Keith asks.

"Me too," I say. "Just a little."

We all laugh, which is kind of amazing, given our situation: three children alone at night, in a snowstorm, in the Arctic wilderness.

"Who wants a story?"

"I do," my brave brothers say in unison.

I start by describing the orphanage where Jane Eyre meets her good friend Helen. I tell about Helen dying. About how Jane becomes a governess and falls in love with her charge's guardian. About the woman in the attic who turns out to be his wife. About Jane escaping in the night. Running through her own wilderness.

"How does it end?" Keith asks.

"Happily," I say.

"Save the ending," Seth says. "Tell it tomorrow night."

Keith makes a sound of annoyance. He wants the ending now, but instead of arguing, he asks, "What's New York like?"

"When we arrive," I say, "the first thing we'll see is the Statue of Liberty. It's an enormous green statue of a woman. She has a crown of spikes, and she's holding a torch high in the sky. In her other hand, she's holding a tablet."

"What's a tablet?"

"It's her journal."

"What's she doing there?"

"She's a symbol of freedom."

"Huh," Seth says, forming his own picture of the Statue of Liberty.

Keith says, "What kind of freedom?"

"Our freedom," I say.

Zhòh stretches and turns in a few circles. He settles back down, now on top of me.

"Oh no you don't." Even if he does provide added warmth, I'm not sleeping with a wolf. I shift him over to the boys' side.

"What kinds of cabins do they have in New York?" Keith asks.

"They have skyscrapers—big tall buildings where people live stacked on top of one another. It's very cozy."

"Does the food there really give you cancer?" Seth asks.

"No." The word *cancer* causes a tremor of fear to zing through me. But the blood has almost stopped. Maybe it's just some kind of short illness.

"Dad doesn't lie," Keith says.

"Of course he doesn't." I pause, choosing my words. "But he only sees a sliver of the whole truth."

"A sliver is just a little bit," Seth says tentatively, as if it has never occurred to him that Dad doesn't have all the answers.

"That's right. How could anyone see all the truth in the world?"

Keith grunts and I take that to be some form of agreement.

"Are there bears in New York?" Seth asks.

"No. Only people. Lots of people, and they're all really friendly."

"What will we do there?"

"We'll go to school. We'll play kickball on the playground."

"What's kickball?" Seth asks.

I describe the game, and answer about twenty questions from Keith, before moving on to trick-or-treating, telling them how every child gets a bag of candy. I also tell them about libraries, where there are entire walls, whole rooms, filled with books.

"I remember Halloween," Keith says longingly.

"Will we eat lots of candy?" Seth asks.

"Mainly we'll eat pizza." I remember Aunt Frances saying that you haven't had pizza until you've had New York pizza.

"What's pizza?"

"It's the best food in the world. It's a big round flat biscuit with tomato sauce and lots of cheese. You can put pepperoni on it, too."

"What's pepperoni?" Seth asks.

"Spicy meat."

"I like meat," Seth says.

"Stop talking about food," Keith says.

"Guess how we'll get to New York," I say.

"Helicopter?" Seth tries.

"Better."

Keith kicks his legs with excitement and shouts, "Airplane!" We see airplanes all the time, flying high in the sky over our cabin, but the only time we've ever been on one was when we flew from Fairbanks to Fort Yukon.

"Yes." I hope I can deliver on this promise.

I reach out and place a mitten against the interior wall of our fort. On the other side of that packed snow are the beginnings of an Arctic winter. Falling snow. Blowing wind. Cold air. Freezing waterways. And we've floated down the wrong creek. We'll have to get our raft back upstream so we can find the real Aurora Creek, and that's going to be hard work. It's going to burn lots of calories. And we have no food.

For now, though, we're warm. We're together.

TWELVE

IN THE MORNING, we squeeze one by one out of the snow-shelter door. The sky is gray, swirled with dark clouds, but the snow has stopped falling and the gale has lessened to a breeze. We overnighted in a sparse forest. Broken tree branches, covered with snow, litter the ground. I pick up a stick and crack it in half. The wood is still autumn dry.

"Where's Zhòh?" Seth asks.

"I heard him leave the shelter earlier," Keith says.

The quiet warmth of our snow fort caused us to sleep late. It's just as well. We needed the rest.

"Zhòh!" Seth cups his hands around his mouth as he calls.

The wolf pup comes running through the trees and

84

sits at Seth's feet. Blood reddens the fur around his mouth.

"You're right, Willa," Seth calls out. "He *does* know how to hunt. Good boy."

"At least someone got a meal," I say.

A snowshoe hare bounds by our camp. Its coat is half dusky brown, its summer color, and half white, its winter color. Zhòh shoots out after the hare.

"Still hungry, I guess," Seth says.

We all are. We need food if we're to continue.

"I'm going to try to get us a ptarmigan for breakfast," I tell my brothers as I fill the pockets of my parka with rocks from beside the creek. "Build a fire."

"But you don't have a gun," Keith says.

"You worry about getting a fire going," I say. "Look under the trees where there will be dry kindling. There hasn't been enough snow yet this year to soak the wood."

"I know how to find dry wood any time of year," Keith says.

"Prove it, then."

Seth begins clearing a patch of ground for the fire, and I set out into the woods, trying to remember exactly what Dad told me about hunting ptarmigan without a firearm. Like the snowshoe hares, ptarmigan are brown in the summer and white in the winter. Now, between the two seasons, they have feathers of both colors. Year-round they forage for seeds and buds, so they tend to sit on branches close to the ground. They're big birds with dim brains. Back when Dad had a sense of humor, he'd joke that they look like they're trying to figure out where they are.

There are plenty of ptarmigan in Alaska. I see one right away. The difficult part will be killing it.

"They don't even know to be afraid," Dad told me. "They don't fly away, if you approach slowly. All you have to do is throw a rock at their heads and knock them out."

The problem is, ptarmigan have tiny heads. You have to have good aim. You also have to be strong. The rock needs to at least stun the bird.

I stand very still and size up my prey. Just as Dad said, it sits there on its tree branch, oblivious. I stalk a few steps closer. Still it sits, blinking its beady little eyes.

Careful to make no sudden movements, I reach into my pocket and close my fingers around a rock. I withdraw it and cock back my arm.

The ptarmigan fluffs up and looks around.

I fire the rock with all my might. It sails a foot to the right of the ptarmigan's head and the bird flaps away.

I soon find another ptarmigan, and this time my rock hits the bird right in the chest, making a little *thud*. Even if my throw had hit the bird in the head, it wouldn't have been hard enough. Discouraged and suddenly more exhausted than I've ever felt in my life, I lean against a tree trunk and want to just give up.

"Willa!" Seth's voice snakes through the cold air, through the tree branches, to my ears. He sounds as if he's miles away, not just a couple hundred yards. But I hear him. My sweet little brother. My charge, along with my other cross little brother. I push off the tree trunk and follow my own tracks back to our camp.

The boys have made a blazing fire. The sight of those hot flames gives me a jolt of strength. I sure wish I had a ptarmigan to cook on them.

"Shh," Seth warns me as I approach.

Keith stands next to a tree, holding the tattered food bag. Seth grips the cool end of a stick from the fire and uses the burning end to soften the pitch on the tree trunk. He uses another stick to scrape up a glob of the gooey hot pitch. He paints the inside of the food bag with the pitch.

"Okay," Seth says. "Put them in."

Keith takes some needles, buds, and catkins from his pockets. He puts these in the food bag, now sticky with pitch. "Ptarmigans' favorite snacks!"

"But what'll make them eat the ones you collected, instead of just getting their own?"

"A big pile in one place is a lot better than having to peck all around the forest," Seth whispers.

"The ptarmigan's feathers will stick in the pitch." Keith speaks loudly, enthusiastic about his brother's inventiveness. "It won't be able to get out."

"If we're lucky," I say, feeling doubtful.

"Shh," Seth says again. "Keep your voices down. You'll scare them away before we even set up the trap."

"We have to put this near the fire so the pitch stays sticky," Keith says, his eyes lit with hunger and excitement. "If the pitch gets cold and hardens, it won't trap them."

"Hopefully they won't be frightened by the fire," I say. Just the thought of roasting ptarmigan meat lights my mind and makes the juices in my cheeks water.

"Actually," Seth says, "our bigger problem is Zhòh. He's off hunting. But if he comes back, no ptarmigan will come near."

Seth sets up his trap with the back end of the sack near the fire. He's threaded a bendy willow switch through the sleeve where the drawstring used to be. He's placed another willow switch circle in the bottom. These two hoops hold the bag open. Seth scatters a handful of needles and catkins on the snow, near the opening of the trap.

My brothers pull me away from the fire and we wait, at a distance of about twenty yards, for ptarmigan. Keith keeps whispering things like, "We have to be ready to seize the bag if one goes in," and, "The ripped bag is weak," and, "Even with sticky feathers, the ptarmigan might be able to work its way out pretty quickly," until Seth hushes him. We stand, eyes pinned on the ratty bag, waiting and waiting.

Keith elbows me hard when a speckled ptarmigan hops into view. It skitters across the snow to the bag and looks inside. I hold my breath.

The bird pecks at the bait scattered in front of the bag. When this is gone, it pokes its beak into the bag opening. The fire pops and the ptarmigan hops a few feet away, turns and stares at the bag, and then hops back. At that moment, somewhere in the not too distant forest, Zhòh howls. The ptarmigan scares off to a nearby tree branch.

Keith groans and starts to talk, but Seth swats him and places a forefinger against his mouth. As I strain my ears, listening for the sound of Zhòh returning, I worry that we're losing precious travel time by indulging Seth's scheme.

All at once, the ptarmigan flaps down off the branch. Hops to the bag. Pushes inside to get the seeds and catkins.

Seth sprints. He grabs the bag by its opening. The willow twig loop makes it hard to close up the top and the bird flaps against the inside of the flimsy fabric. Seth fumbles and the bag falls to the snow.

"Get it!" Keith shouts.

"You do it!" Seth yells back.

The ptarmigan is vocalizing and thrashing.

Keith runs and snatches the bag. He manages to shake the bird down to the bottom and closes his fist around the fabric just below the top willow hoop. "What now?"

We all know what now. We also all know that, even though we're starving, neither I nor Seth can do it.

Keith walks the bag over to a tree trunk. He swings the bag to the side and with all his force—

I look away but can't help hearing the dull *thud* of the bird hitting the tree trunk. When I look back, the bag is motionless.

We are still, too, for a moment, realizing the miracle of breakfast.

I send up a cheer and do a little dance right there in the snow. When I stop twirling, I see, sitting in a tree branch not ten feet from me, another ptarmigan. This one must be extra-dumb, because even my cheering and twirling hasn't startled it.

I take a rock from my pocket, cock back my arm, and fire.

The rock hits the bird right in its head. It falls to the ground.

"Keith!" I can't bear to touch the scaly little legs or feel the oily feathers. "Get it!"

Here comes Zhòh, running at full speed, headed for Seth. But when he sees the fallen bird, he changes course.

Zhòh and Keith arrive at the same time, on either side of the stunned but not dead ptarmigan. The wolf pup closes his jaws around the feathered bulk. Keith backs up, looking over his shoulder at us. Seth runs to his pup. He crouches down and says, "Drop it," as if the wolf were a trained house dog.

"Don't!" I cry out as Seth reaches for the ptarmigan still in Zhòh's jaws. Coming between a wolf and meat is as dangerous as coming between a brown bear sow and her cub.

Even from where I stand, I can see Seth and Zhòh gazing into each other's eyes. Zhòh widens his jaws and lets the ptarmigan fall to the snow. He backs up several steps and lowers his tummy to the ground, his paws stretched in front. He whines.

"Thanks, Zhòh," Seth says, and he picks up the twitching bird. To his brother he says, "It's not dead yet."

Keith hands the bagged ptarmigan to me and takes the stunned one dangling from Seth's hands. A moment later it, too, is dead.

"Good boy," Seth says to Zhòh, and scratches the pup behind the ears.

It takes us well over an hour to pluck the birds. My hands shake from hunger, but we work next to the fire so we're warm enough. I make sure we have very sharp, sturdy sticks for roasting. We can't afford to lose a single morsel.

I let the boys choose the parts they want. Keith starts with a leg, Seth with breast meat, and I spear another hunk of breast meat. I hold the stick over the fire and listen to the sizzle and hiss as the meat browns. My stomach wrenches with hunger, and it takes a lot of willpower to not eat it raw. But the wait is worth it. The roast ptarmigan is succulent and flavorful. We lick our fingers. We scrape our teeth along the bones. Then we break the bones and suck out the marrow. I even sneak a bit of roasted meat to Zhòh.

Strength courses into my arms and legs. My brain feels as if it's been turned on again.

"You guys are awesome," I say.

"You too," Keith says.

"Yeah, you too," Seth agrees.

I figure this is a good time to tell them about my

mistake. I explain that we've floated down the wrong stream and that we're going to have to go back. I brace myself for their reaction, but with meat in their stomachs, the boys take the news in stride. They wade upstream in the shallow creek, their high rubber boots keeping their feet dry, dragging the raft. I wade behind, pushing, and Zhòh trots along the shore. We reach Sweet Creek by early afternoon.

We climb on board with Zhòh and begin floating once again. Not even an hour later, we come to the confluence of a much larger tributary. This, I am sure, is the Aurora Creek turnoff.

I look around to get our bearings. Sweet Creek spills into the bigger waterway, both streams slate gray, a few shades darker than the sky. I can practically see the ice crystals in the air. The water is a degree or two warmer than slush. The surrounding trees hold their loads of snow from last night's dump. From this intersection, I can't see any mountains at all, and I miss them, their stalwart show of strength. It's just dark, flowing water, endless snowy forest, and the three of us.

THIRTEEN

DESPITE ITS NAME, Aurora Creek is wide, fast-moving, and deep. Our raft swirls in the churning mix of currents at the meeting of the two waterways. I jab the steering pole, trying to gain purchase, but it no longer reaches the bottom. The current sucks us right out into the deep flow. We speed along, at the mercy of the rushing water.

"Good," I say to the boys. "Nice and fast. We'll be at Fort Yukon soon."

"Soon?" Seth says, his voice reedy with worry.

I look into the distance, as if I can almost see the town. The sun is low. A flock of geese fly overhead in a V formation. Their wings flap against the deepening sky.

"If we don't stop for the night, we'll get there faster."

"How will we know when we're there?"

"It's a town. There'll be lights."

Seth puzzles what this looks like.

Keith says, "But how will we even get the raft to shore?"

I'm saved from answering this question by a faint rumbling. The sound scares me at first, as if the earth itself is letting out a low growl. Motion in the sky, over the trees to the east, catches my eye.

A helicopter. My mind skids on the enormity of what this means. Helicopter means people. People mean rescue. The chopper changes course and heads in our direction. The pilot has spotted us.

For a moment, the idea of being rescued, being safe, fills me with relief.

But what if it's Dad? He probably would have left the moment he got back from hunting. He would have rowed all night, not even stopping to sleep. He may well have passed us up while we were sidetracked on the wrong stream. He could have gotten to Fort Yukon ahead of us.

We are dead center in the pilot's sights, three children and a wolf pup coursing along on a rustic raft in the middle of a swift river. Dad might be looking at us through a pair of binoculars right now. When the helicopter is almost overhead, the pilot banks the chopper so it flies almost sideways. He's dropped so low that the wind off the propeller blows our hair.

The boys huddle on our raft, Keith with his hands over his head and Seth with his face buried in Zhòh's neck fur, but I kneel, my head craned back, and gape at the people in the chopper. It's not Dad. Besides the pilot, there are two passengers, a man and a woman, both wearing knit hats and big parkas. They look like a couple of flight-seeing tourists. They point and stare at us.

I know the international signal of distress, standing and waving my arms up and down. The pilot would be obliged to call the authorities in Fort Yukon. A rescue team would be dispatched. They'd give us food. I could see a doctor about my bleeding. Tonight we'd sleep in beds. My brothers would be safe.

And . . . we'd be returned to Dad's custody.

He'd take us back to the cabin on Sweet Creek. With his drinking, anger, and failing dream. And the long, dark days of winter.

I stand up and give the pilot the A-OK sign by making a circle with my thumb and forefinger, the other three fingers splayed up. I force a smile and wave him off, communicating that we're just three Alaskan kids out on a lark.

Sure enough, he banks his helicopter and flies off toward the interior.

I check the boys' faces to see if they're okay with this decision. Keith clenches his shoulders and touches the bruised place on his jaw.

"He'll hurt Zhòh," Seth says, understanding my silent question.

"I want pizza," Keith says.

"Okay, then," I say. "New York, here we come."

FOURTEEN

"WHAT IF THE pilot radios back to town?" Seth asks. "We're in plain sight on the river if someone comes looking."

"He won't, though," I say. "I signaled that we're fine."

"We're fine," Keith barks, as if repeating it will make it so.

"But if Dad reports us missing—"

Seth is right. We're so obvious rafting down this river. But it's by far the fastest way to travel and without food and shelter, we need fast. I interrupt the questions by singing in a loud voice: "Pole, pole, pole your raft, gently down the stream."

The boys gawk at me, and then glance at each other. Dad taught us to sing the original version of this song when we first arrived at Sweet Creek and he was building our rowboat. I point at Seth when I get to "merrily," and he shrugs and joins in with, "Pole, pole, pole." Next I point to Keith, who is wearing his fiercest scowl, but he surprises me by also joining in at the right place. We sing the round three times.

Next I start in on one of Mama's favorite songs, "Red River Valley." The boys don't know this one—Dad wouldn't want me to sing it around him—but I remember all the words perfectly. They learn the verses and tune quickly, and we sing it through twice.

"'Down by the Banks of the Hanky Panky,'" Keith suggests, and Seth sings the first lines by himself:

Down by the banks of the Hanky Panky,

Where the bullfrogs jump from bank to banky.

Right on top of the small raft, speeding along the river, Seth tries to get up to do the hops and claps that go with the song. He falls back down, and even Keith laughs.

Just as we start in on the second verse, a loud *creak* interrupts our singing. A sharp *crack* follows as one of the raft's outer deck planks pops up off the foundation logs. Seth wiggles the plank with the toe of his boot. "This board is wonky. The nails are rusted."

"Worse," Keith says. "Two of the foundation logs are separating."

We all stare at the wobbly plank, and then at the widening gap between the planks, as the raft slides into a rougher patch of the river. The wavelets bounce us along until an eddy snatches the raft and swirls it in a swift circle. The plank and logs loosen even more. I quickly check how far we are from the riverbank— too far.

"Deck," Seth recites. "Hull. Bow. Stern. Oars. Rudder."

"What are you talking about?" Keith says.

"Back when Dad was building our rowboat, Willa showed us that picture in the encyclopedia that named all the parts of boats."

I'm surprised Seth remembers this, but Keith lights up. "Yes! If we had a rudder, we could use it to steer the raft to shore."

I grip the bad plank and wag it back and forth, like a loose tooth, until I am able to yank it off the logs.

"Even better than a rudder," I say. "A paddle."

As the bad side of the raft starts to sink, we drag our packs to the high side. Zhòh barks at the water as if he can scare it away like he did the bear. I kneel on the tipped deck and dig the plank into the water, pulling hard. We slide a bit toward the riverbank. I stab my makeshift paddle back into the water, pull again.

All three of us, our packs, and the pup crowd the

high end of the raft. Again and again, I plunge the plank into the river and pull as hard and fast as possible. When the raft sinks farther into the river, Zhòh leaps into the water and swims to shore. He shakes himself off and yips his encouragement.

My knees feel like they're breaking. My arms and back strain with the paddling. But it's working. We're within striking distance of shore.

Keith jabs the steering pole into the river and hits bottom. Seth starts singing, "Pole, pole, pole your raft," as Keith pushes with all his might.

But a countercurrent grabs the raft and pulls it back out toward the center of the stream. All my work is about to be lost with one swift play by the river. The foundation logs separate even more as another plank pops loose.

Keith rips off his parka and hauls off his boots and jeans.

"No!" I bellow.

"You can't swim!" Seth yells.

Keith slides into the river, keeping his hands on what's left of the raft. He pants for breath as the frigid water seizes his thin torso. Holding on with both hands, he manages to work his way around to the back. From there he kicks his skinny legs. I paddle with the board. Seth pushes with the pole, quietly singing.

"My feet are touching bottom!" Keith yells a few seconds later.

He pushes us the rest of the way to shore.

Seth and I toss the packs, as well as Keith's boots and clothes, onto land and jump off the raft. Keith collapses in the mud like a half-dead muskrat. His long underwear is soaked and he's shivering hard. As he tries to stand, his legs buckle.

"Quick," I say to Seth. We each support a side of Keith, holding him up by the armpits. "Into the trees."

Once we get off the riverbank, into the forest where we'll be out of sight, we drop Keith on a dry patch under a tree.

"Fire," I tell Seth. "As fast as you can."

I hustle back down to the water's edge. Hesitating only a moment, I put a foot on what's left of the raft and give it a shove into the river. It drifts and spins on the current. With any luck, it'll sink soon. There'll be no sign of us whatsoever if the chopper pilot contacts any authorities in Fort Yukon.

I pick up our stuff and, stumbling over the shoreline rocks, carry everything up to the forest. Keith is shivering violently. As Seth kneels to light the kindling he's gathered, I strip off my pants and long underwear, and quickly put my pants back on. Keith takes off his wet clothes and puts on my dry long underwear. I spread out the tattered plastic tarp and throw our zipped-together sleeping bags on top. While Seth builds up the fire, I climb into the sleeping-bag pouch with Keith so my body heat can warm him up.

After about thirty minutes, Keith stops shivering and starts talking, recounting the details of his swim. I take the cooking pot to the river, fill it, and then tuck this next to the fire. Soon we're all drinking hot water to warm us up. It's almost dark and I'm too exhausted to build another snow fort, so I get back into the sleeping bags with Keith, and Seth joins us.

"You said you'd tell us the ending to *Jane Eyre*," Seth says, amazing me that he can think of stories at a time like this.

"She almost died." My voice is weak and hoarse. "She wandered around in the wilderness, hungry, tired, and cold. But she never compromised on doing what she knew was right."

I wait for one of the boys to ask, *What is right?* But we all pass out.

FIFTEEN

I WAKE UP at first light. When I climb out of the sleeping bags, the air is so cold it feels like my bones will crack. I stuff my feet into my boots and shake the boys awake.

Seth sits up. "Where's Zhòh?"

"I don't know. Please just pack up. Let's go."

"But—"

"No arguing. We need to make tracks."

"He's probably hunting," Keith reminds Seth. "He won't be far. He'll find us."

I wrap Keith's frosty long underwear in the shredded tarp and stuff this lump, and the sleeping bags, into the packs. The trick will be to stay in the woods, where we can't be seen by boats on the river or helicopters in the sky, but close enough to the creek so that we can follow the shoreline.

A ways past our camp we enter a clearing scattered with camping debris. In the dim light of early dawn, I make out buckets, two camp chairs, strewn beer bottles, and a big bear-proof food locker. Embers still glow red inside the fire ring. From the big tent comes a loud, rumbling snore.

We all stare for a moment until I jerk my head to the side, meaning that we need to keep moving. But Keith heads for the food locker. I wave my arms in a big X over my head, trying to stop him. He unlatches the bear-proof lid.

"Keith, no," I say as loudly as I dare.

A man's voice in the tent mumbles something.

After only the briefest pause, Keith turns back to raiding the locker. He grabs candy bars and packages of jerky. He stuffs as much as he can in his pockets. He tosses more to Seth, who looks at me and, even though I vigorously shake my head, holds on to the food. The crackling of candy wrappers sounds extra-loud in the early-dawn stillness.

I gesture for them to stop, to come on, *now*.

The snoring grows louder, and more irregular. Two big *snogs*, and then silence.

I run to the food locker as silently as possible and try to drag Keith away from the cache. The long tent zipper opens.

"What the heck?" The man's rumbling voice sounds sleepy.

"I'm sorry," I cry, trying to take the food from Keith's hands. "We'll give it all back."

Unbelievably, Keith twists away from me, wearing his defiant face.

The man grunts as he shoves out of the tent and stands. He has long stringy hair and a big belly. "I thought you was bears."

"I'm sorry," I say again. "Seth, Keith, put it back."

"You little thieves." The man gestures at Keith's stuffed pockets and Seth's armful.

"Apologize," I say to my brothers.

"Sorry!" Seth shouts but Keith tears the wrapper off a candy bar and takes a bite.

"We're leaving now," I sputter. "Keith. Put the food back."

"They have a whole locker of food," Keith says. "He's already fat."

"What?" the man says, slitting his eyes.

"He said he's very sorry."

A younger man, with shaggy hair and a big mustache,

emerges from the tent, holding a rifle. "Who are they?" he asks.

The gun scares the boys into finally dropping most of the food on the ground, though Keith stuffs the rest of the partially eaten candy bar in his mouth. Just then Zhòh trots into the clearing. He stops, looks around, and starts yapping.

"That a wolf?" asks the big stringy-haired guy.

"He'll attack anyone we tell him to attack," Keith says.

The young guy laughs and points his rifle at Zhòh.

"No," Seth cries.

Gripping the boys by their arms, I drag them away from the camp.

The gunshot tears a hole through everything.

I drop onto the ice-crusted soil, covering my head with my arms. Keith and Seth topple next to me. Pain courses through my bloodstream, flows everywhere, but it's a general pain, not a bullet-hole pain. I squeeze a fistful of frozen leaves. I'm alive. I roll over and check each of my brother's faces. Terrified, but they're alive, too.

"For crying out loud, Lloyd. You just shot at *kids*."

"Nah," Lloyd says. "I shot at the wolf."

Seth lunges to his feet and screams, "Zhòh!"

"Zhòh!" Lloyd imitates in a falsetto voice, and laughs so hard he has to bend over and hold his knees.

I scan the clearing but don't see a wolf corpse.

"Let's go," I say quietly to my brothers. "Come on. Please."

"Zhòh," Seth sobs again, but both boys follow me out of the clearing, trailed by the men's laughter.

We walk along the edge of the forest in silence, keeping Aurora Creek in sight. A wind whips the shiny gray surface of the river, making small whitecaps. A thick cloud cover, heavy with moisture, hangs low in the sky.

"Wait," Keith whispers. "Listen."

A familiar rustling scamper. Followed by a yip. A moment later, the pup is running toward us, his pink tongue hanging out the side of his mouth, his hot breath steaming the air. We all drop to our knees to hug Zhòh. Seth scratches his ruff and promises him all the meat he wants when we get to Fort Yukon.

Then Seth tearfully attacks me with a hug. I gesture for Keith to join the hug and he does. "Don't you ever steal again. Do you understand?" I brush Keith's long, tangled hair out of his face. "I know you're hungry. But there is no situation, ever in life, when stealing is a good idea. Do you hear me?"

"You promised pizza," he says, as if that has anything to do with stealing.

"I asked if you heard me."

Keith nods. "When do we get pizza?"

"Say, 'Yes, I hear you.'" I sound like Dad. But I'm about to take these boys into civilization. If they steal there, bad things will happen to them.

"Yes," Keith says, "I hear you."

"Good. It's not far." Once again, I try to sound confident. "Just a few hours."

"Piece of cake," Keith says, using one of Dad's expressions.

"I'd like a piece of cake," Seth says.

"What flavor?" I ask as we all start walking again. There's actually a trail now, through the sparse forest and following Aurora Creek. That means we're getting close.

"Zucchini," Seth says.

I laugh. "Just wait. When we get to New York, you'll learn about caramel and strawberry and vanilla."

"We already know about chocolate and cinnamon," Keith says.

"You won't believe the possibilities," I say, and for a moment, I feel it: a big blooming hope.

Aurora Creek widens, the flow breaking into five channels, separated by gravel bars. As we pass through another spruce forest and emerge onto a large stretch of grassy tundra, we see at last the confluence of the Aurora with the mighty Yukon River.

SIXTEEN

A **LIGHT SNOW** begins to fall again as we walk. We pass into an aspen forest, the sky visible through the naked branches. A flock of migrating geese honk and flap overhead. For a while we follow lynx tracks on the trail.

"Zhòh would like a lynx kitten," Seth says. "For a friend."

"You mean *you'd* like a lynx kitten for a friend," Keith says.

"Yes," Seth agrees.

In the early afternoon, I tell the twins to go ahead and that I'll catch up. Once they're out of sight, I quickly empty my bladder, noticing with relief that there is no more blood. Just to be safe, I put another gauze patch in my underwear, and then run to catch up. The boys sit on

110

a fallen log, gaping out at the river, waiting for me. Even though they're so skinny, their bodies look heavy with exhaustion. I hope we can reach town before nightfall.

Keith picks up a rock and tosses it toward the river, as if to prove he still has strength. Seth begins to copy his twin, choosing a stone and cocking back his arm, but he freezes mid-throw.

I follow his gaze upriver.

From this distance, it's just a speck on the water. But it's a moving speck, full of intense energy, dark against the light gray surface of the river, open to the massive sky overhead.

A rowboat. I can see the rocking motion of the rower, leaning forward as he dips in the oars, and then backward as he pulls them through the water, over and over again.

Robert Slone-Taylor once told me that your whole life passes before your eyes in the moment before you die. It feels just like that now, only not my whole life, just my life with Dad. Riding on his shoulders. Maple-walnut pancakes. The alpine blue in his eyes as he reads stories. Felling trees for our cabin. Stuffing the seams of the rowboat with tree pitch. And more recently, burning my journal. Shooting a rifle into the sky. The sickening sound coming from the woodshed.

Keith runs down to the water's edge. He raises his arm, about to beckon Dad to us.

I understand. Dad looks so lost, rowing hard in the cold northern air, bucking the wind and waves, alone, desperate. He probably rowed all night.

But I won't go back. Not now, after all we've been through to get this far. I won't stand by while he continues to drink. Continues to hurt Keith. Forgets about our education. Lets us starve to death over the winter. I won't do it.

If the boys want to flag down Dad, I can't stop them. But I'm heading for New York.

I run back into the forest and crouch down in some thick brush where I can still see the river but can't be seen. The boys understand their choice. In unison, they look over their shoulders at me. Still in unison, they look back at Dad rowing down the river. Finally they look at each other and make one of those twins decisions where they don't even have to speak.

Like puppies, with Zhòh at their heels, they skitter up the rocky embankment, running to join me in my hiding place. Together we watch as Dad grows bigger and bigger. Soon we can see his long, thick black beard and his red fleece hat, both dusted with snow, his strong arms working the oars, rowing as if his life depended on it.

"He's going to kill us," Seth whispers when Dad is directly across from us.

"He'll get to Fort Yukon before we do," Keith agrees.

"Shh," I say, even though Dad is at least fifty yards away. We watch as he rows right by on the big wide river. Soon we see only his back, his strong rowing rhythm, the clunky homemade boat mowing through the Arctic water as he grows smaller again. We wait until he is out of sight.

Seth takes my hand. Even Keith leans against me. My legs feel wobbly.

"Here's the plan," I say, making it up on the spot. "We'll find a hiding place outside Fort Yukon. Somewhere we can stay until I can get us plane tickets for New York."

"He'll find us," Seth says.

"How will you get plane tickets?" Keith asks.

"Let's walk," I say, my mind buzzing with their worries and about twenty more of my own.

SEVENTEEN

JUST AS I think I can't take another step, I see through the trees what looks like...yes, it's a cabin. We could stop and ask for food, but we're so close, and I can't risk us being turned in to the authorities.

Soon there's another cabin, and yet another.

I want to kiss the ground. We made it.

Fort Yukon looks much like it did five years ago. The settlement sits on the banks of the Yukon River, but the surrounding area is called the Yukon Flats. My brothers and I avoid being seen by walking through the trees above town. We pass through a grove of birch, the bark papery white and only a few of the brilliant yellow leaves hanging on. The snow falls right through the branches. But on the far side of town I find a cluster of spruce.

Their branches form a thatched roof, catching the falling snow, leaving a cozy nest of dry spruce needles on the ground beneath them. I settle the boys and Zhòh in the spruce fort.

"I'm going into town. Do not leave this spot, even for a second. Do you hear me? I need you to do exactly as I say."

"What about Dad?" Seth asks. "He'll be in town by now. He might see you."

"That's why I'm going alone. Three of us would draw attention. But I can sneak around on my own."

"What will you do in town?"

"Find a phone and call Aunt Frances." I don't tell them that I don't even have her phone number.

Seth nods and cuddles Zhòh. But Keith announces, "I think I should go."

"No."

"But—"

"I'll be back in a few minutes with food."

That's the magic word. Keith mumbles, "Okay."

I push my hair up under my fleece hat, pull it down to my brow, and set out.

The town lies between our fort and the river. So wherever Dad has tied up the rowboat will be on the other side of the buildings and streets. Where would he go first? Maybe to the police to report us missing? He might not have thought about the raft because it's been out of sight from the cabin for over a year. He'll probably think we're on foot, that we're still in the wilderness. He won't be looking for us in town.

Entering on a side street, I keep close to the buildings and try to walk like a boy, the whole time watching out for Dad. When I spot a pizza shop, all other plans fly from my mind.

The guy who works behind the counter doesn't look up from his phone as he asks for my order. The smell of hot baking dough, tangy tomato sauce, and luscious melted cheese almost causes me to pass out.

"A pepperoni pizza, please."

"What size?"

"Extra-large."

He puts in earbuds and keeps talking on his phone while he makes our pizza. A few minutes later, I have in my hands a big box wafting delicious aromas. I pay the guy and rush back to the hiding place.

As I duck into our fort and flip up the cardboard top of the pizza box, Keith gulps and Seth sucks in his breath. They both grab slices, long strings of cheese stretching from the box to their mouths as they bite into the pizza. Keith shouts, "Good!" and tomato sauce squirts out the side of his mouth. Zhòh licks the splat off his boot. I take my own piece and close my eyes. It's just the way I remember it, with gooey cheese, zesty pepperoni, and a chewy crust.

It's our happiest time since leaving the cabin. The snow falls thickly now, weighting the branches over our heads, but we're warm and dry. The boys agree that pizza is the best food they've ever eaten. Zhòh enjoys his slice, too. I tell them again that New York is filled with pizza shops.

New York! Seeing the pizza shop made me forget all about calling Aunt Frances. It's just as well. Night might be a better time for sneaking around town. I'll go back in a couple of hours, under the cover of darkness. The stormy weather will help hide me, too.

We unfurl our sleeping bags in the nest of spruce needles and get in together. The boughs are just inches from our faces, and I breathe in the wintergreen scent. It feels so good to be safe and warm, with a hot meal in our bellies. I fall asleep and don't wake up until morning.

Crawling on my hands and knees out of our fort, I find Keith standing a few yards away, hands on his hips. Snow covers the ground but the sky has cleared.

"I'm going into town to find Dad," he says.

"Let me call Aunt Frances first."

"I want to talk to him." Keith scowls, looking out at the horizon. I do understand what he's feeling. The pull to Dad, to everything we've ever known, is so strong.

"But then what?" I ask.

He scowls harder.

"I'll tell you what. Back to the cabin. We'll never go to school. I'll never have a best friend."

"I don't want to go to school. You don't need a best friend. You have us."

"I'm asking you to do this for me. To wait. To let me call Aunt Frances. Please, Keith. For me. If after I call Aunt Frances, you want to go back with Dad to the cabin, well..." I can't quite let myself finish that sentence. I can't let Keith go back. So I say, "I'll get us another pizza."

"Pizza!" Seth calls out.

Keith hesitates but finally says, "Okay. We'll stay here. Just until you call Aunt Frances."

I leave him standing there, staring out over the tops of the trees, scanning the horizon, and hope he stays put.

I don't know how to disguise myself any better, so I decide to use speed to avoid being spotted. I run the whole way into town where I find out that the pizza shop doesn't open until noon. But there's a grocery store. A man sits behind the cash register, and next to him on a tall stool is a bright-eyed girl with black hair pulled back into a ponytail, and two dimples on either side of her smile. I pick out a package of donuts and a carton of milk and set them on the counter.

"Anything else?" the man asks.

I shake my head and keep my eyes down.

"That's not a healthy breakfast," the girl says. "The milk is good for you, but you shouldn't eat doughnuts for breakfast. Even on a Saturday."

Saturday. How funny to think about the days of the week. That's why this girl isn't at school, I guess.

The man laughs and says, "Amelia, mind your business."

As he hands me my change, he says, "Visiting?"

"Yes," I say. "My family and I are going hiking." It's sort of true.

"Pretty late in the season for a hiking trip," he says. "Freeze-up any day now."

"My dad is super-experienced." Also true.

A loud *crash* in the back of the store draws their attention away from me.

"Susie? You okay?" the man calls out, and then hurries over to the accident.

"Dad's new employee," the girl says cheerfully. "This is the third time she's broken stuff."

A phone sits on the counter right in front of me. I could

ask the man to help me find Aunt Frances's number. But he's already asked too many questions, almost like he's suspicious. I don't know if Dad has put out the word about us around town yet. But even if he hasn't, when the man overhears my phone conversation, if I'm even able to reach Aunt Frances, he'll for sure turn us over to the authorities. For now, it's best to go back to the hiding place, and fast. I run out of the store. As I jog down a side street to keep out of sight, I hear footsteps following me.

"Hi!" the girl calls out. "Where are you going hiking?"

Amelia's wearing high-top sneakers, blue jeans, and a red sweatshirt on top of a gray one, but no parka, despite the cold. A big smile warms her face.

"Go away." I feel mortified for speaking so sharply. I'm almost growling.

She holds her hands in the air and says, "Sorry. Just curious, is all."

"Sorry," I mumble.

"Where are your parents? Are you camping?"

This girl looks so lighthearted and clean, so full of inquisitiveness and vigor. Her family has a grocery store, and she gets to hang out there with her dad. She probably has a mom, too. She has an entire town to call her own. I don't want to lie to her.

Clutching my doughnuts and carton of milk, I run.

By the time I reach our tree fort, I'm breathing hard and crying, too. I throw the doughnuts at Keith and drop the carton of milk next to Seth. They open the packages and, seeing how upset I am, try to give me a doughnut and a drink of milk. I shake my head and tell them to eat.

"Hello? Hellooo." I recognize the girl's voice, but can't see her because we're hidden under the tree boughs.

"Don't shoot!" she calls out, laughing. "Okay, I admit it, I followed you."

"Who is that?" Seth whispers.

"My name is Amelia," she says.

I feel ridiculous hiding, so I scoot out from under the spruce boughs and stand facing her.

"I don't think you're on a hiking trip," she says. "Who are you?"

"That's none of your business," Keith says, ducking out of the fort. Seth comes out, too.

"I need to call New York," I blurt. "Do you know how I can do that?"

"*New York?*"

"Our aunt is there," Seth says.

She squints. "What are your names?"

I push the boys in back of me. "We're not saying."

Amelia's smile fades. She twirls her ponytail between her thumb and two fingers.

"Don't tell your father," I say.

"But—"

"Please."

She works her mouth back and forth, and then fixes her gaze on Zhòh. "Where'd you get the wolf pup?"

"I tamed him," Seth says.

She nods, still twirling her ponytail. "Wait here, okay? I have an idea."

"I need you to promise that you won't breathe a word to any adults about us."

She frowns, but nods, and sets off at a run.

Fifteen minutes later, Amelia returns. She pulls three peanut butter sandwiches from a paper bag and hands them out to us.

"Healthy breakfast," she says.

The boys snatch the sandwiches and start scarfing them down.

"So look what else I have." She takes a phone out of her pocket. "It's my mom's. I sort of borrowed it. I have to get it back soon, before she starts looking for it. What's your aunt's number?"

"I don't know the number," I whisper.

"Hm. We can try directory assistance. Here, I'll do it. What's your aunt's name?"

"Aunt Frances," Seth says.

"Yeah," Keith says.

Amelia rolls her eyes and gives me a conspiratorial smile about the silliness of little brothers.

"Frances Moore," I say.

"There might be a few of them in New York," Amelia says, tapping on the front of the phone. Holding the phone to her ear and speaking in an adult-like voice, she says, "May I please have the number for Frances Moore?" She covers the phone with her hand and says, "She has two in Brooklyn and three in Manhattan."

"New York," Seth says.

"They're parts of New York City," Amelia explains.

"Manhattan?"

"Manhattan," she says into the phone. She listens for a moment, and asks me, "Does she have a middle initial?"

My hopes sink. How would I know?

All at once, a memory pops into my head: Mama and Aunt Frances are bent over laughing in our Seattle kitchen. "Chloe Maude!" Mama shrieks her own name. "Frances Zelda!" Aunt Frances calls out hers. "Why did they give us such old-fashioned names?"

"Z!" I shout.

"Her middle name is Zhòh?" Seth asks, and then laughs.

"Hush," I tell him.

"Z," Amelia tells the operator, and her eyes light up as she says, "Thank you." She hands me the phone. "The operator is connecting you."

As I hold the phone to my ear, my heart pounds so hard I think it might knock me down. I haven't figured out what to say. I'm almost glad when a recorded message says that she is out right now and that callers can leave a message. I'm so nervous, I drop the phone.

Amelia picks it up. "What happened? Voicemail?"

"It was her recorded message."

Amelia nods. "We could leave a message—"

"But Aunt Frances would call back and your mom would know you took her phone."

"Well, yes, but—" Amelia looks at the phone as she talks.

"No," I say. Amelia's parents would call the authorities, who would turn us over to Dad. "You promised not to tell your parents."

"Okay. I'll come back later today and we can try again. I have to go now. Dad's on the Tribal Council. He has a meeting at ten. Of course Mom has to watch the store, so I have to watch my little brothers." She grins. "I have *three*."

Amelia takes off at a run.

EIGHTEEN

"WILL ZHÒH LIKE New York?" Seth asks.

"I don't think I'll go to New York," Keith says. "I'm staying in Alaska."

"I don't think he *will* like it," Seth says, petting his wolf. "The food is unhealthy."

"Yeah, besides, there aren't any trees."

Here they go again, quoting Dad. I try to distract them with stories of how fun New York will be and how kind Aunt Frances is. I'm winging it, pretty much making things up as they come into my head, while we wait for Amelia.

The sun has reached its zenith and already started to shift westward when I hear the rustling of boots moving through leaves. Next I hear the low, sonorous tones of a man's voice.

Dad.

Zhòh raises his nose and sniffs the air.

I put my hand on the trunk of the spruce tree and feel its dry, scaly bark. A long drip of sap, the tree's blood, runs down next to my hand. The spruce's roots spread out into the earth. Its branches stretch high into the sky. How can a living thing be both rooted, stuck in one place, and reach for something entirely new at the same time?

I come out of our fort, bracing for Dad's wrath.

But the man who steps into our spruce grove isn't Dad. It's the grocery store man, along with a pretty woman and Amelia, who calls out, "I'm sorry! I'm sorry!"

"Hi, kids," the woman says.

"Howdy." The grocery store man smiles. "Wow, you're right, Amelia. They *do* have a wolf pup."

Zhòh runs in circles, as if unsure about whether he needs to protect us from these new intruders.

"I'm sorry for telling," Amelia says. "But Mom and Dad are really nice and they left the store with Susie—the one who knocked over that display when you were there?—and so they don't have much time but they really wanted to meet you. It's going to be okay. I promise."

The man puts a hand on Amelia's shoulder to quiet her tumble of words.

The woman has three plastic mugs and a thermos. She puts the mugs on the ground and pours out hot tea. She hands us each a steaming drink.

Keith slurps down the hot tea. I tell him to say thank you, but he doesn't. Seth cradles his mug and blows on the surface to cool it. I can barely hold on to mine, I'm so overwhelmed by my expectation of seeing Dad and the surprise of these people.

"Let's have a chat," the grocery store man says. Most of the snow has melted, but he sits right in the damp forest leaves. The woman sits, too.

"Are you the one who had a Tribal Council meeting?" Seth asks.

"Yes, little man, I did. And I'm thinking—"

"Fort Yukon is home to the Gwichyaa Gwich'in people," Seth interrupts. "Is that you?"

The man throws back his head and laughs at Seth's excited questioning. "That's us."

"It means 'people of the flats,'" Seth says, as if Amelia's family doesn't already know this.

The man smiles warmly and says, "You're a well-informed young fellow, aren't you?"

"Robert Slone-Taylor told me. He has a Gwich'in

dictionary. It was written by Clarence Alexander and his wife, Virginia. He was chief from 1980 to 1994."

"A fine man."

"You *know* him?"

The man laughs again. "Fort Yukon is a small place and Clarence is a big man. He's my mentor and hero, actually."

Seth is practically glowing with excitement. "Robert Slone-Taylor told me he founded the Yukon River Inter-Tribal Watershed Council. They're working on making sure the rivers all stay clean. And in 2011, President Barack Obama gave him the Presidential Citizens Medal. Did you get a medal, too?"

Still chuckling, the man shakes his head. "Listen. Why don't we have our own Tribal Council meeting. Have a seat." As we all sit in a circle, the man winks at Keith, who is looking skeptical. "I'm Amelia's dad. Stanley Johnson. You can call me Stanley. This is her mom, Constance. Amelia did the right thing and told us about you kids."

"I wanted to bring my brothers, too," Amelia says. "So you could meet them. But we left them with our neighbor. They're too little to understand."

"We know your father," Amelia's mom says. "He comes to town every year for supplies." Stanley and Constance exchange a look, one that hides a secret, something they're not saying.

"He stayed in town extra days this summer," I say, guessing the secret.

"Yes," Constance says.

"Do you know where he is now?" I ask.

"He arrived yesterday," Amelia says. I can tell she wants to be the one telling the story, but her mom puts a hand on her knee to shush her.

Stanley says, "He thought you kids would still be much closer to your cabin, nowhere near Fort Yukon yet. A search team left this morning, flying along the route they thought you'd have taken."

"They didn't find us," Seth says.

"Nope," Stanley says.

"How'd you get here so fast?" Amelia asks.

"We rafted," Keith tells her.

"Wow," she says. Again, her mom taps her knee so Stanley can go on.

"So when Amelia told us your whereabouts, we decided to tell your dad that you're safe, but not where you are. We thought we'd have a chat with you first."

"He agreed to that?"

Amelia's parents exchange that look again.

"Here's the deal," Constance says. "Amelia told us you

tried to call your aunt, so the number is on my phone. I went ahead and called her again. She'll be here tomorrow afternoon."

"Aunt Frances?" I whisper. "She's coming? *Here*?"

"Yes," Constance says.

"We have lots to talk about," Stanley says. "We thought you could come to our house for the night. When your aunt gets here tomorrow, we can talk with her and your father."

"Dad's really good at problem-solving," Amelia puts in. Then she repeats, "He's on the Tribal Council."

"I want to see Dad," Keith says.

"I understand," Stanley says. "But it'd be better to wait until tomorrow. Let's go. We can put your pup in the backyard."

"You won't shoot him?" Seth asks.

"Shoot him!" Amelia cries out. "My dad would never do something like that!"

"He's a wolf," Stanley says. "He's not meant to live with people. But I can promise you I won't shoot him. Or let him go, either. He's probably too tame now to get by on his own."

"I'm sorry I told," Amelia says again, twirling her ponytail with her fingers. "I know I promised not to."

"It's not good to break promises," Constance says. "But it's also not good for children to be on their own. You made the right decision, Amelia."

"We're fine on our own," Keith says. "We have all the skills we need."

"I can see that," Stanley says. "You are very able children."

"Come on back to the house and get warmed up and have something to eat," Constance says, getting to her feet with a grunt. She holds out her hands. "Willa. Seth. Keith. Come with us?"

They know our names.

"You really talked to Aunt Frances?" I ask.

"I did. She's so worried about you kids, but Amelia told us you're doing fine, so we told her that. She can't wait to see you."

We shoulder our packs, but Keith hangs back as we walk through the woods to Amelia's family's cabin. I keep expecting him to take off at a run to look for Dad. But I guess the prospect of food does its trick because he stays with us.

The Johnsons' place is a small blue house surrounded by a big yard with scruffy grass and patches of mud and snow. Stanley puts Zhòh in the fenced backyard, promising Seth that he'll be safe, and then heads back to the store. Constance hands out clean, fluffy towels and we take baths. Amelia gives me a tub of coconut-lime hand cream. She says it's her favorite scent and that I can keep the whole tub. I rub a big glob into my chapped hands. She also gives me clean leggings, a T-shirt, and a fleece zip-up. Her little brothers—Eddie, Carl, and Zachary—are only three, five, and seven, so the Johnsons don't have any clean clothes big enough for Keith and Seth. Constance runs our clothes and sleeping bags through the washer and dryer while the boys sit wrapped in blankets. It feels like a miracle that I don't have to scrub their jeans with stones in icy creek water.

At dinnertime, all nine of us squeeze around the table and have big hot bowls of moose, carrot, and potato stew in a rich gravy. After that, we have apples baked with cinnamon and honey, dolloped with vanilla ice cream. The boys don't remember ice cream at all, and their eyes practically roll to the backs of their heads in bliss. All through dinner, the three little Johnson boys ask us question after question about our journey. My brothers exaggerate the details in telling about the bear, the big river's strong current, and Keith's plunge to guide the raft to shore, as well as Zhòh's acts of valor on our behalf, but they aren't lies, just elaborations. The twins are thrilled to have an audience.

Before bed, Stanley reads us two stories from a book of folktales. Amelia makes faces at me, as if we're too old for stories. But I love listening to Stanley read. I can't believe we're warm, that our bellies are full, that we have a roof over our heads, that Aunt Frances is coming.

Constance puts my clean sleeping bag on a foam pad on the floor in Amelia's room. She spreads Keith's sleeping bag, plus one of theirs, on the couches in the front room. My brothers haven't slept in a room by themselves for five years, and both boys look scared. I gather them in a rough hug and whisper, "I'm right here, just on the other side of that door." I nod toward Amelia's room. Keith wiggles out of the hug, but Seth stays for a second or two longer.

Lying in the dark, Amelia tells me her favorite color is orange and that she's going to be an astrophysicist. I've read the encyclopedia articles about stars, so I know that starlight comes from stars that are already burned out, that red giants are old stars, and that a supernova is the explosion of a star. I tell her that I might be an astrophysicist, too. Amelia says that we can have an observatory together.

I take a deep breath and say, "I think I'm sick."

"Oh no. Are you going to throw up?"

"No. It's . . . I mean . . . blood."

"You're bleeding? Where? Should I get a Band-Aid? I'll call Mom."

"No! Um. Not like that. It stopped. But it was in my..." I'm too embarrassed to say more.

"Wait. You mean you got your period?"

I don't know what she's talking about.

"Was the blood in your underpants?"

I nod but realize she can't see me in the dark, so I say, "Yes," the word coming out a squeak.

"Oh, Willa. That's probably just your period. I started six months ago. It's kind of obnoxious, all that blood every month, but oh well, that's life, right?"

"Um..."

"You know what your period is, right?" When I don't answer, she says, "Oh, wow, I mean, I know you don't have a mom. I'm really sorry. That's probably why you don't know. She would have told you. Every girl gets her period. The blood comes once a month. It's part of having babies."

"I'm having a baby?" The words strangle my voice.

"No! The bleeding, your period, means you *can* have a baby. It's just biology."

"I thought...I thought I had some disease."

"No way! It's normal." She explains everything to me and I feel so relieved I cry a little bit. She says, "Some of the words make me laugh. *Uterus. Fallopian tubes.* They sound like the names of planets." Before long, I'm laughing, too.

Next she tells me what her mother has told her about sex. We start laughing so loud we snort.

"Girls!" Constance shouts from another room. "Sleep! Now!" Which makes us laugh even harder.

NINETEEN

I WAKE SOME time in the night to the sound of my brothers whispering. For a second I think I'm in our cabin up on Sweet Creek. Then I remember. I'm on the floor in Amelia's bedroom in the Johnsons' house in Fort Yukon. I hear Seth say, "Keith, no!"

Footsteps clunk across the front room floor—booted steps, not barefoot ones—and the door opens and closes. Dressing as quietly as possible, I shoot out of Amelia's bedroom to see what's going on.

"Keith left!" Seth says. "He says he's going to find Dad!"

"Stay here. I'll get him."

Out on the Johnsons' porch, I catch my breath. Overhead the northern lights swirl in brilliant shades of lime green and magenta. Like genies, the colors burst and expand, swoop and jiggle. All at once, they become bars of light, with purples and blues joining the pinks and greens in a dance across the entire sky. I know the dazzling light show is caused by collisions between electrically charged particles from the sun. The northern lights are my favorite thing in the Arctic, and whenever I see them, I feel as if my own body is filled with the bright billowing colors. They feel like a celebration.

I don't want to chase Keith. I want to go back to sleep, to talk with Amelia in the morning, to eat more good meals and take more hot baths. Maybe Keith just needs to run.

"Willa," Stanley says, coming out the door behind me, "where's your brother going?"

"Seth says to find Dad."

Stanley sprints after him. I expect him to tackle my brother, drag him back by the scruff of his parka. Instead he trots alongside Keith. They slow to a walk. Stanley doesn't touch Keith, but I can hear his voice, talking, talking, talking. They stop. Turn. They start walking back this way.

I don't know what Stanley has said to Keith, but it must be true that he's a good problem-solver, because he has managed to turn the problem of Keith around.

Back inside, Seth is already asleep again in his sleeping bag on the couch. Constance has set a pot of hot tea on the table, alongside plates of pilot bread, butter, and smoked salmon strips. Keith sits right down and helps himself.

"Middle-of-the-night snacks are my favorite kind," Constance says, putting a mug of tea in front of him.

"I'll have some of that," Stanley says, pulling out a chair and sitting on the far side of the table from Keith. He continues speaking to Constance as he says, "Keith wants to talk to his father, which is exactly the right response to the situation." Turning to Keith, he says, "How about we stick with the plan and wait until tomorrow?"

"Where is he?" Keith demands.

"I don't know where he's camping," Stanley says. "Somewhere in the woods."

"But you said you've talked to him," I say. "Where did you see him?"

No one answers me. Keith and I both stare at the adults, waiting. When they don't speak, I say, "I saw a liquor store in town."

Constance nods.

"He'd been sober for years," I say, suddenly wanting to defend him.

She nods again.

Stanley sighs and says, "That makes sense with what we saw this summer. Your dad's always been a loner. He'd come to town each year, get supplies, barely talk to anyone, and get right back up to your cabin. I guess he wanted to avoid the liquor store, avoid temptations. There isn't a tavern in town, but a guy who has a cabin on the outskirts hosts parties that can last a few days." Stanley makes air quotes around the word parties. "I was surprised when I heard this summer that your dad had joined that group. Anyway, I had a pretty good idea that's where I'd find him yesterday."

"And you were right?" I ask, wanting him to be wrong.

Stanley nods.

Keith scowls, but grabs another smoked salmon strip and takes a big bite. He chugs back the rest of his tea.

Watching Stanley and Constance with Keith, how good they are at getting him to do whatever they want him to do, I have a new thought. What if I don't have to be in charge anymore? I go stand at the window and look out at the pulsating electric-blue and royal-purple, fireweed-pink and spring-green sky. Tonight's northern lights display is the most magnificent I've ever seen.

"Hey, you know what?" Stanley calls to my back. I listen without taking my eyes off the sky. "There're lots of stories about the northern lights. My favorite one says that the lights are torches carried by spirits to guide nomadic travelers."

I swing around. "Really?"

"Yep. Kind of cool, isn't it?"

I look back out at the northern lights, which have become subdued into washes of pale green, and consider letting them guide me now.

TWENTY

—✦—

"SHE'S HERE!" AMELIA whoops. "Oh my goodness, look at her!"

The boys are watching cartoons on the TV, transfixed by the pictures and voices and story. I'm standing in the middle of the living room, about ten feet back from Amelia, who's at the window.

"Come quick," she says, beckoning me with big hand motions.

It's late afternoon but still light out. I can see her perfectly: Aunt Frances. She's walking up to the Johnsons' front door between Constance and Stanley. She's plumper than I remember, but has the same long, curly brown hair. A sparkly clip holds it off her face. She wears a long black down parka with fake-fur trim and puffy boots, which look more like big slippers, and are already covered with mud. She tiptoes up the walkway, holding her hands in the air, as if she's afraid that the wild environment will swallow her.

Amelia elbows me and whispers, "Glamorous."

I can't stop staring. The voluminous hair. The sparkles. Bright lipstick. It's like she's three people bursting out of one. She's both beautiful and frightening.

Amelia elbows me again and says, "I can't wait to hear her talk. How do you think people in New York talk?"

The boys tear their eyes away from the TV and get up from the couch to stand behind me, each one holding on to a handful of my T-shirt, both breathing loudly.

"You should go greet her," Amelia says.

"Wolves greet by touching noses," Seth says.

"We're not wolves," I say.

Amelia howls quietly, "Ah-ooooooo!" She pulls me by the hand toward the opening door. I tow the boys, who don't let go of my T-shirt. Aunt Frances pushes right past Constance. She wraps her arms around me and bursts into tears. Being hugged by Aunt Frances feels like being squashed by pillows.

"You're so big!" she cries out. "And brave! And beautiful! You look just like Chloe at this age. Oh, oh, oh!"

She dives at the boys and they both startle at first but then hold extra-still, like animals in a trap, while she hugs them. She keeps saying, "Oh, oh, oh!"

She removes her gloves and tosses off her black coat, revealing a woolly red sweater and tight jeans with rhinestone designs on the pockets. Her fingernails are painted the color of raw salmon flesh.

"Do you want to meet Zhòh?" Seth asks.

Everyone stares at him, amazed. You just never know what Seth is going to do. Here he is being the one who talks first.

Aunt Frances looks a little confused but says, "Of course I do."

"He's in the backyard." Seth heads to the door off the kitchen, and the rest of us follow.

"Maybe just from the porch," Constance says, but Seth charges out into the yard.

"Come, Zhòh!" The pup scampers across the muddy weeds and leaps onto Seth, pawing his legs and whimpering with pleasure. Seth says to Aunt Frances, "You can pet him if you want."

Aunt Frances catches her breath. She looks at Constance, who shrugs, and then at Stanley, who lifts his hands as if to say, *It's your call.* So she bites her lip and begins tiptoeing into the yard. Keeping a good distance away, she bends at the waist and extends a hand toward the wolf pup. Maybe it's the long, salmon-colored fingernails, but Zhòh lets out a low growl and backs up a few steps.

The rest of us crack up. Aunt Frances whirls around and laughs herself. "Well, gosh, we don't have wolves where I come from."

Constance says, "Come on back inside. I'll get dinner started while you kids talk with your aunt."

Stanley corrals the four Johnson kids to their bedrooms to give us some privacy, and then he leaves to help Susie close up the store for the day. Aunt Frances perches on the edge of the couch and the boys stand gaping.

"Close your mouths," I tell them.

"Sit, kids. Let's have a good long talk."

The boys don't move but I sit on the far side of the couch. I'm still staring, amazed. I know telephones can call anywhere in the world and that airplanes go hundreds of miles an hour. Still, how did she get here? Mama's sister. Right in front of me. All bursting and sparkly.

"Tell me everything," she says. "Start from the beginning."

I can't imagine what would constitute the beginning.

I study the four corners of the room, trying to figure it out, while Keith jumps right in. Soon he's joined by Seth. The boys tell her the entire story of our escape, from commandeering the raft to hiding in the spruce fort. She covers her eyes at the brown bear part and takes hold of my hand as they tell her about the hunters with the rifle.

"Willa, your mother would be so proud of you."

I flush hot. "For what?"

"For bravery. For taking care of your little brothers and knowing how to pluck ptarmigans and build fires and make forts to sleep in. For—"

Keith interrupts her. "Everyone knows how to do those things."

"No," Aunt Frances says. "They most certainly do not."

"Would our mother be proud of us, too?" Seth asks.

"Oh, my, *yes.*"

"For taking care of Willa," Keith says.

"That's just the start of it," Aunt Frances agrees.

"I thought Dad was coming with you," Seth says.

"He'll come a bit later." Aunt Frances purses her lips.

"Is he angry?" I ask.

"Well...I'm not sure how to answer that question."

"He's at some cabin drinking," Keith tells Seth, who was asleep during last night's conversation.

"Like cocoa? Or lemonade?" Seth wants everything to be sweet.

"Seth," Keith says. "Why do you ask questions you know the answers to?"

"No," Aunt Frances says. "Like whiskey."

"How do you know?" Seth asks.

"We stopped and visited with him," Aunt Frances says. "On our way here from the airstrip."

I'm suddenly angry. White-hot angry. Dad keeps us to the strictest bare-bones existence, and yet he's indulging himself. Hanging out with people. Drinking. He's choosing whiskey over us.

"Does he even care that we ran away?" I shout.

"Oh, sweetie, yes. He rowed all day and night, not even stopping to sleep, to find you. But when he learned that you were safe, the stress was too much for him. He just let go."

"Let go of *us*?" Seth asks.

"Heavens, no. He let go of himself." Aunt Frances takes a deep breath. She scoots across the couch and puts an arm around me. She extends her hand and wiggles her finger at my brothers, asking them to come closer. They don't. They hover on the far side of the Johnsons' front room like two skittish mule deer. Aunt Frances says, "Your dad's a mess, I'm not going to hide that from you."

Keith and Seth lean against each other. They don't understand. No one ever told them, because they were too little when Mama died, about how Dad had quit drinking. They only know what they've seen since July.

"I'm not one to endorse drunkenness," Aunt Frances continues. "But just this one time I was kind of glad he was so sauced because it made him talk. I learned a lot."

She pauses too long and so I press. "What? What did you learn?"

"Your father's a man of strong convictions."

I already know that. "Go on."

"He's still pretty adamant that the wilds of Alaska have everything you need."

"He read my journal. About my wanting so many things we don't have at the cabin. He doesn't care."

"He cares, Willa."

"But—?"

Aunt Frances just shakes her head. Even the adults don't have answers.

"Doesn't he want to see us?" Seth asks.

"Of course he does. But the Johnsons told him he wasn't welcome here in his present state."

"He didn't drink at all," I tell Aunt Frances, "until this summer. He brought whiskey back from this year's supply run."

She nods. "When your mama died, I think he thought he could beat the grief by coming up here. But grief always catches up, one way or another."

The boys just stare, wide-eyed. I want to tell Aunt Frances about so much more than our journey, but don't know where to begin.

"I told your dad I wanted to take you three back to New York with me."

"What did he say?"

"He said no."

My heart sinks. That was my plan. My only plan.

"But we can continue the conversation," Aunt Frances says. "Stanley told him he's welcome to come over to talk, any time he's sober."

"Dinner is ready," Constance calls from the kitchen door.

Aunt Frances gathers me, Seth, and Keith in a hug. "I just love you guys. I can tell that you're super-resilient."

"What does 'resilient' mean?" Seth asks.

"It means I have so much confidence in your abilities to handle everything you need to handle."

We don't all fit around the dining room table anymore, so Amelia and I sit on the couch and hold our plates in our laps. She keeps whispering comments to me about Aunt Frances and about her parents, funny observations that make me laugh. The boys finish their food in about five minutes. It's already dark, but Stanley flips on the backyard floodlights so they can run out to play with Zhòh. Being with a regular family, talking and joking and playing, feels really good.

TWENTY-ONE

WE'RE ALL STILL sound asleep when someone bangs on the Johnsons' front door. Amelia and I come out of her room as my brothers scramble to their feet. "Who the heck?" Constance says, following Stanley into the living room. The Johnson boys run out of their room, too.

"Charles," Stanley says, opening the door. "Good to see you. Come on in."

"Where are my children?"

My brothers hold my hands as we walk over to face Dad. His eyes are bloodshot, and the skin around them darkened. His posture is stiff, as if everything hurts. Dad looks at all three of us for a long time before speaking.

"You ran away. You called Frances. Why'd you do it?"

150

I can't find my voice.

"You hate our life that much?"

It's not what I hate. It's what I want. But I still can't find the words.

"Are you hungry, Charles?" Stanley asks. "How about some coffee?"

He shakes his head. "Get your gear, kids. Let's go."

"At least come in for some breakfast," Stanley suggests. "Before you all leave."

"Do you mind?" Dad says, raising his voice. "I'd like to talk to my kids. Alone."

"Say what you need to say," Constance says. "With us here."

Dad glares at Constance but doesn't argue.

"Why'd you do it?" he asks again.

He read my journal. He knows the answer, at least some of the answer, to his question. I whisper, "I want to go to New York. I want Keith and Seth to come with me."

Dad looks out into the dark, as if there's something important just beyond the Johnsons' yard. "We can walk back to the cabin," he says, ignoring what I just said. "It'll be an adventure."

"Charles, for heaven's sake," Constance says. "The rivers are freezing."

"I said walk, not row."

I know my dad could do it. He could walk all the way back to the cabin, even at this time of year. He'd love it. He'd build snow shelters every night, manage to catch enough snowshoe hare and ptarmigan along the way. He could probably even get us three kids there, if not comfortably, at least alive.

"We could go back in a helicopter," Seth suggests.

"Flat-out broke, son. Our savings are gone. I can't hire a pilot. But that's okay. Good, even. This is when our skills will be truly tested. How about it, kids?"

I feel both of my brothers' grips tightening on my hands. I shake my head no.

Dad takes a couple of deep breaths. He nods hard once, making a decision. "Okay. Fine. Go to New York with your aunt for the winter. I'll stay here in town. Get a job. Make a little cash. We can go back to the cabin in the spring." He pauses and looks almost apologetic. "Fresh start after the melt."

"Sounds like a plan," Stanley says.

"Nobody asked you," Dad says, before loping down the path to the front gate. There he stops and turns, looks at us gathered under the porch light for a long time. Without another word, he disappears into the early-morning dark.

TWENTY-TWO

AT BREAKFAST, STANLEY says, "I made some phone calls and found a home for Zhòh."

Seth doesn't miss a beat. "Zhòh is coming to New York with me."

"That's not possible," Stanley says. "He's wild. He needs miles of wilderness for roaming."

"He's tame," Seth says.

"Not far from here, a woman named Charlotte has a sanctuary for wolves. Ones exactly like Zhòh, who have been tamed by humans, and then abandoned."

"I would never abandon Zhòh!" Seth shouts. He runs for the back door, as if he is going to collect his pet wolf and leave on his own, right this minute.

Constance jumps up and intercepts him. She holds

Seth in a tight hug as he thrashes. Amelia widens her eyes at me and I shrug. Seth shrieks, "Zhòh is coming to New York! Zhòh is coming to New York!"

Stanley says, "I used the wrong word. Of course you'd never abandon Zhòh. But I know you'd want to choose the very best life for him."

I'm glad Aunt Frances is still at the guesthouse the Johnsons found for her. If she saw Seth's behavior, she might change her mind about taking us back to New York.

"Seth," Constance says, "wait until you see the city. It's all buildings and paved roads, millions of people everywhere. Zhòh would be so unhappy. A sanctuary where he can—"

Seth puts his fingers in his ears.

Stanley tells the rest of us that the sooner Zhòh is integrated into his new pack, the better he'll adapt, so we'll be taking him later today. After breakfast, the three older Johnson kids head off for school and Stanley goes to open the store. Constance, Eddie, who is too little for school, my brothers, and I pick up Aunt Frances and we have a tour of Fort Yukon and its surroundings. Aunt Frances keeps gasping, as if it's the wildest place she's ever been. When we spot a brown bear, she practically faints, even though it's a couple hundred yards away and we're in the van.

After lunch, I pretend I'm watching television with the boys, but really I'm listening to Aunt Frances talk to Constance as she makes arrangements for our flights to New York.

"Do you really have to go *tomorrow*?" Constance asks. "You know the kids are welcome here for however long."

"I work as an office manager in a medical clinic. My boss didn't appreciate my taking off with no notice. I really do need to get back. Besides, I don't trust Charles to not change his mind. The sooner we go the better."

"Charles is in pretty bad shape," Constance says. "I'd be very surprised if he pulls it together anytime soon. Are you prepared to keep the kids for good, if it comes to that?"

"Of course," Aunt Frances says.

New York. For the rest of my life. Is that what I really want?

Shortly after three o'clock, when the other kids get home from school, Stanley leaves the store with Susie again and we get ready to take Zhòh to the sanctuary.

We use a piece of meat to lure him into a wire crate and load this into the back of the van. Tears stream down Seth's cheeks and he refuses to go with us. Keith stands close to his twin and says he's not going, either. So Constance and Aunt Frances stay with the boys, while Amelia and I go with Stanley to take Zhòh to his new home.

Amelia and I sit in the middle seat, leaving Stanley by himself in front. He pretends he's our taxi driver and calls us *mesdames*, which Amelia says is French for ladies. As the van bumps along the dirt road on our way north, I can't quite believe how fast the miles disappear under the tires. Until today, I haven't been in a vehicle since we got out of Dad's truck in Fairbanks five years ago. I feel carsick as we go around the curves. Or maybe I'm just feeling sick from seeing Dad this morning. Will he be okay here on his own?

But Amelia makes me laugh by telling stories about her little brothers. I tell her stories about mine, too. It's not long before we're laughing at everything we see out the windows: a man wrestling a wild turkey, a cloud in the shape of a woman's body, a ramshackle house with moss on the roof so thick trees are growing out of it.

The more we laugh, the more we can't stop. *Everything* is funny. A big airy happiness, like the high atmospheric pressure preceding good weather, lofts inside me.

When we get to the wolf sanctuary, we park in the gravel parking lot and jump out of the van. A woman with short blond hair and a big smile comes out of the cabin next to the entrance. She holds out a hand to Stanley and they shake. He introduces us to Charlotte.

"How about a quick tour?" she asks. "So you can decide whether this would be a good home for your wolf."

Stanley and Amelia wait for me to answer, so I say, "Okay."

We climb into Charlotte's truck and, while a volunteer holds open the big gate, she drives us into the fenced wolf sanctuary. The volunteer closes the gate behind the truck.

Charlotte drives slowly along a dirt road that winds through the sanctuary and tells us about wolves in zoos who've bitten zookeepers and must be given new homes. About wolves rescued from roadside attractions where they were kept on short chains. Or ones bought illegally from breeders as puppies and kept in small cages, even after they reached adulthood. Charlotte has a deal with the Department of Fish and Game: before euthanizing a problem wolf, they are supposed to call her. Sometimes they do, and sometimes they don't. The nineteen wolves in her sanctuary have homes for the rest of their lives. They can run and play in the forest. They get regular meals. They have each other for a pack. As we roll across the sanctuary acreage, we spy two gray wolves and one white wolf.

"We have a program for veterans, too," Charlotte says. "It's been really successful."

"I didn't know wolves did military service," Stanley jokes, and Charlotte smiles.

Amelia says, "Dad. Please."

"We pair up sanctuary wolves with returning vets," Charlotte says. "When you think about it, they're going through a lot of the same things. Trauma. Loss. Rediscovering the meaning of home and family. Experiences that most people in their lives can't fully understand. The vet develops a long-term relationship with one of the sanctuary wolves. Each relationship is unique, depending on what the wolf and the vet need, or can handle. But we've found it to be really healing."

Dad isn't a veteran. But he might need a wolf partner, anyway. I would pair him with the white wolf. They have the same bright blue eyes.

When we get back to the cabin at the entrance gate, Charlotte asks, "Do you think Zhòh will be happy here?"

"Yes," I say. "I'm sure of it."

Amelia helps me wrestle the cage, with Zhòh inside, out of the back of the van. We each weave our fingers into the wire sides and crab-walk the load to the sanctuary gate. Charlotte unlocks it and we carry the cage into a smaller fenced area where the new arrivals are released.

She explains that Zhòh needs to be kept separate from the other wolves for a while, until they decide to accept him. Stanley stands outside the enclosure, arms crossed, letting us handle the release of the wolf pup.

I bend down and unhinge the cage door. Zhòh looks up at me.

"He's so pretty," Amelia says.

I take a long look, memorizing the picture of his thick gray coat, the sweet white mask around his eyes, the white legs and the white tip on the end of his tail.

"He saved our lives," I say.

"All the wolves save our lives," Charlotte says. "We need top predators in the food chain to keep the ecosystem healthy."

"Why isn't he leaving the cage?" Amelia asks.

"Give him time," Charlotte says.

"He's just a puppy." I hear myself repeating Seth's words.

"I have another pup," Charlotte tells us. "Maybe six months older than Zhòh. A female. He'll have a young one to play with."

"A girlfriend." Amelia grins.

Zhòh shoots out of the cage, runs straight for the perimeter of the fenced area. He does a full lap and flies back to me. He stops and yips. I scratch behind his ears and tell him, "I love you. Seth loves you. Keith, too! We'll love you forever. You be a good boy, okay?"

Off he runs again. This time he stops at the side of the enclosure nearest the forest and pokes his nose through the fence.

"If the space observatory doesn't work out for us," Amelia says, "we could have a wildlife sanctuary."

"Yes!" I agree.

Charlotte locks the gate behind us, and Stanley carries the empty cage back to the van. As Amelia climbs in, she says, "Driver, take us to Fort Yukon."

I hold back and look for a long time into the trees of the wolf sanctuary, thinking of the white wolf, the two gray ones, and all the others I didn't get to see. I whisper, "Goodbye, Zhòh."

A low moan rises out of the trees. Followed by a higher-pitched howl. Three or four, even more, wolves all sing out at once. Zhòh lifts his chin, nose pointed at the sky, and howls. He has met his new pack.

TWENTY-THREE

WE GET UP in the dark, well before dawn. I hoist my pack and leave the house. My brothers and the Johnson family follow. As we head to the van, I check for the northern lights, but the sky is solid black behind a sparkle of stars. It's so cold that I can practically see the feathery white frost in the air.

We all stuff into the Johnsons' van, with me sitting next to Amelia in the middle seat. My brothers and I have to hold our packs in our laps. When Stanley turns on the van's heater, Seth gasps at the blast of warm air. The idea of not having to chop wood or build a fire in order to be warm seems almost like magic. I reach back into the seat behind me and brush the hair off his forehead. "The van has a heater," I whisper.

Amelia elbows me gently and smiles. Last night I told her she didn't have to get up at this horribly early hour to drive to the airstrip with us.

"You mean vomit o'clock?" she'd said. I finally find a friend—one who understands little brothers and wolves, one who likes to talk and wants to have a space observatory, one who loves the color orange and makes me laugh—only to have to leave her, move thousands of miles away.

"What about Dad?" Keith blurts.

"Will he meet us in New York?" Seth asks.

"He's staying here," I say, and pause to clear the jiggle from my throat. "You boys heard what he said."

We pick up Aunt Frances from the guesthouse, and ride out to the Fort Yukon airstrip, all of us as silent and glum as the predawn darkness. When we arrive and get out of the van, a stiff wintry wind blasts my face. The lake bordering the western length of the runway is entirely crusted over with ice. A couple of ragtag buildings squat next to the runway, and a bright orange wind sock puffs out from its tall pole. I wonder if I'll ever see Amelia, Stanley, Constance, Eddie, Carl, and Zachary again.

"Don't cry!" Amelia shouts. "I always cry when other people cry." She laughs and wipes away the tears running down her cheeks. "We'll e-mail. It'll be fun."

I open my pack and dig out *Jane Eyre*. I hold it out to her. "A present."

She tips the book, trying to read the title in the fading starlight. "Is it good?"

"It's so good."

"Thanks."

"Let's go, girls," Stanley calls. He, Constance, Aunt Frances, and the boys have gathered at the bottom of the set of stairs placed on the tarmac next to the airplane door. "The plane takes off in fifteen minutes."

Just a ten-seater, what Stanley calls a puddle-jumper, the little plane will take us to Fairbanks. From there we'll board a much bigger plane for flying to New York.

Amelia puts her arm through mine and squeezes. "New York," she whispers. "You'll see the Statue of Liberty."

New York has been like a mirage, a dreamy floating picture of friends, books, pizza, and playgrounds pulling me forward. But it's no longer imaginary. I'm going there. To the real place, not the mirage. There will be whole herds of kids. Soaring buildings instead of mountains. Whooshing traffic instead of wind. People as thick as mosquitoes in July. I may be resilient, but I might not know how to talk to city girls. I'll be so far behind in school, I'll be the dumbest one in the class. In the

Johnsons' bathroom mirror, I saw how raw I look, like some kind of prehistoric girl, with my ragged hair and a crooked tooth.

Suddenly I miss our cabin, the stream, the birches and spruces, the blue daytime sky and starry nighttime sky. Was it only a few days ago that I crouched behind those bushes on the banks of the Yukon River and watched Dad row by?

As Amelia and I join the group, a tall man with a handlebar mustache steps down from the plane and introduces himself as Hank the pilot. He starts loading our luggage onto the plane. I'm still fighting tears.

Stanley's phone trills.

"At this hour?" Constance says.

Stanley retrieves the phone from his pocket. "Huh. That's strange. It's Charlotte."

"Charlotte?" Seth asks.

"Hey, Charlotte. What's up?" Stanley listens for a long time. "I see. Uh, no. Not yet, anyway." After another listen, he says, "Can I call you back later this morning? Okay, good. Talk soon." He clicks off his phone.

"What?" Seth demands.

Stanley claps his hands. "Okay, kids, let's get you on that plane."

Seth yanks his arm. "Why did Charlotte call? Is Zhòh okay?"

"Yeah," Zachary says. "Why did she call before dawn?"

"It's dawn now," Stanley says, and waves an arm at the sky, midnight blue instead of black, the stars no longer visible. An icy cloud cover is sweeping in from the north.

Keith steps up to Stanley, his chest practically touching the man's stomach, and says, "It's not right to conceal information."

"Keith," Aunt Frances says.

"No, no, he's right," Stanley says, rubbing his jaw. He steps around Keith and puts a hand on top of Seth's head. "Son, a volunteer accidentally left a gate open. Zhòh got out last night."

"You said he'd be safe!" Seth yells, and bursts into tears.

"I'm so sorry. But I bet they'll find him."

"Find a *wolf*? Doubtful," Keith says.

"Listen," Stanley says. "Charlotte called right away this morning because she thinks Zhòh might come back to Fort Yukon. Animals always circle back around to home."

"This isn't his home!" Seth sobs.

"No, but it's the last place he was with you," Stanley says.

Seth stamps the hard tarmac. "You said he didn't have the skills to make it on his own! He's only a pup!"

"Seth. Please stop." Aunt Frances crouches next to him. "We'll call the Johnsons as soon as we get to New York, and I bet Zhòh will have been found by then, safe and sound, back with Charlotte. We need to get on the plane now."

Keith points a finger at Stanley. "You said he'd be safe at the sanctuary."

I imagine Zhòh running wild through miles of forest, drinking from streams, afraid, alone. Dad, too, is wild, alone, maybe even afraid.

Hank ducks out the open door of the plane and stands on the top step. He raises a hand and says, "Time to go, folks!"

The decision hits me like a gust of Arctic wind.

"We're not going," I say.

Aunt Frances looks shocked.

"I can't leave Dad. He's not well."

"Willa," Constance says, "we're going to try to enroll him in a substance abuse program in Fairbanks."

"I'm sorry," I say to Aunt Frances. "You flew all the way out here for us."

"You don't have to take care of your little brothers

anymore," she says. "And certainly not your father. I've got it from here."

I shake my head.

"Look," Aunt Frances says, "I know you're scared. But a girl who can ward off grizzly bears—"

"We call them brown bears," Amelia corrects.

"A girl who can ward off brown bears, navigate Alaskan rivers, and build snow forts will be able to handle New York. Trust me."

I shake my head again. She's right. I tackled all that. But I only did it so I could save my family. The job's not done.

"I'm not going, either," Seth announces. "I won't leave Zhòh."

Aunt Frances looks out at the gathering storm and wraps her scarf more tightly around her throat. She's desperate to get on that plane. Raising her voice, she says, "Enough. Hop on board. *Now.*"

"I'm sorry, Aunt Frances. But we're not going."

Keith drapes an arm around Seth's neck in solidarity. I stand behind both of them.

The rising sun bursts through an opening in the clouds. Copper light slices through the blue cold, lustering the ice on the lake.

"Hey!" the pilot shouts from the door of the plane. "Last call. Weather coming in. We have to shove off." He disappears inside the cockpit. The plane's engine roars to life.

"Okay," Stanley says. "Frances, you go on. We can keep the kids for a few days. We'll talk when you get to New York and make a plan. We'll figure it out."

Aunt Frances glances at the frozen lake, the orange wind sock now billowing at a ninety-degree angle, and shudders.

She holds me by the shoulders and asks, "Are you sure?"

When I nod yes, Stanley says, "You kids go back to the van. I'll get your luggage."

I wait to watch Aunt Frances climb the plane steps. She looks so weary, as if that short flight of stairs is a mountain pass. Then I herd my brothers away from the plane. Constance, Amelia, and the Johnson boys follow us, and we all pile into the van. A minute later, Stanley arrives with our luggage, which he dumps back onto our laps.

Seth starts humming. Constance coughs. Stanley turns the key in the ignition four times before the van starts.

Amelia cries out, "Hey! Look!" She laughs her big loud laugh.

At first I think she means the tiny snowflakes

dancing in the freshening wind. But then I see the dark shape approaching and realize it's Aunt Frances's long black parka. A second later, she opens the van door, shoves her suitcase under my legs, and gets in.

"What say I treat everyone to breakfast," Aunt Frances says. "There *is* a café in this town, right?"

"Waffles!" Zachary hollers from the front seat.

"I want a cinnamon roll!" Carl says.

"Cheesy scrambled eggs!" Eddie chimes in.

Aunt Frances looks at me. "What?"

"You got on the plane. I thought you were leaving," I whisper. My hand clamps down on her shoulder, as if to hold her in place.

"I had to tell that tall pilot we weren't coming. I also tried to negotiate getting our money for the flight back."

"You're a brave woman," Constance says with a smile. "I'm glad you're here."

"Did that work?" Stanley asks. "The negotiating part?"

"Well." Aunt Frances smiles. "Hank seems like a good fellow. I can't say we came to an agreement this morning. But we started a dialogue."

"What's a dialogue?" Carl asks.

"Talking," Zachary says.

"But what about your flights from Fairbanks to New York?" Stanley sounds alarmed.

"The only kind available on short notice were the expensive refundable ones," Aunt Frances says. "So we're covered."

"I'm sorry, Aunt Frances," I say.

She smiles at me. "It's not your fault. Moving on to plan B."

"What's plan B?" Seth asks.

"The *next* plan," Amelia explains. "After plan A."

Aunt Frances's voice shakes a little as she says, "I'll call my boss and ask for a couple more days off."

"Flexibility is always good," Constance says.

"Especially where kids are involved," Stanley adds.

"If you say so," Aunt Frances says, heaving another giant sigh. "I'm starving. I'm going to go with the cheesy scrambled eggs *and* a cinnamon roll."

"I don't have a plan B," I say quietly to Aunt Frances.

"Neither do I," she says, and gives me a hug. "Yet."

The snow is coming down more thickly now. The light is a frigid silver. As we drive away from the airstrip, I look over my shoulder and see our small plane, a winged smudge of gray through the falling snow, soaring into the sky.

TWENTY-FOUR

"THERE REALLY ISN'T time for breakfast at the café," Constance says as the van bounces down the road toward town. "The kids will be late for school."

"There's time if we hurry," Stanley says. "It takes the boys about two and a half minutes to finish off a plate of food."

"Who's going to open the store?"

"I'll open it a little late."

As Stanley and Constance quietly argue, Aunt Frances looks out the window and I hear her moan softly. "How long does the snow last?" she asks.

"At least six months," Zachary answers. "Usually longer."

She moans again, this time loudly.

"Here," Amelia says, and hands me *Jane Eyre.*

"But I gave it to you."

"I know. I'm not giving it back, not for keeps. But maybe you need it now."

"How do you know that?"

"The pages are so worn they're like tissue. The cover is hanging by a few shreds. Obviously you've read it a million times."

I slide the book into my parka pocket, keeping one palm against its cover. If I've learned anything from Jane Eyre, it's that nothing is ever completely lost. You just keep looking. You just keep surviving your losses. You figure out the next steps.

When Stanley parks in front of the café, we all get out. The boys are so noisy, no one hears me at first. I raise my voice and repeat, "I'm skipping breakfast. I'm going to see Dad."

"There's plenty of time for that later," Stanley says.

"I have to go now."

"But it's snowing," Aunt Frances says.

Constance laughs and puts an arm around Aunt Frances. "I think Willa can handle snow."

"But how do you even know where he is?" Amelia asks.

"I have a pretty good idea," I say.

The three adults exchange looks. Stanley scowls. Aunt Frances shakes her head.

"Half an hour," Constance says, putting a hand on Stanley's forearm when he opens his mouth to object. "Can we agree to that? You'll be back here at the café in half an hour?"

"I'm going, too," Keith says.

"Me too," Seth says.

Stanley puts an arm around each of them. "Seriously? You want to hike through more snow and wind and cold instead of sit in a cozy spot eating a hot breakfast?"

They follow him right inside, trailed by Constance and Amelia, who looks over her shoulder at me and smiles encouragingly.

As Aunt Frances steps toward me, I straighten my spine, thinking she's going to argue against my going to find Dad. Instead she says, "I'm proud of you, Willa. You've grown up so fast, and I sure like the person you've grown up to be."

I want so badly to follow her through those doors, order a plate of bacon and eggs, pretend I'm part of the Johnson family, snuggle up next to Aunt Frances. But I still have the last, the hardest part of my journey to finish. I nod, turn, and walk away.

I head for the river, which is wide and braided through this region with many channels, islands, and mudflats. In other words, a million places a man could tie up a rowboat. At water's edge, I look in both directions. The snow is whiting up the landscape. The temperature has plummeted, so the flakes are dry and powdery. The entire river is crusted over with ice this morning. Freeze-up. Today. Right now.

A couple hundred yards upriver, I see the dark shape of a rowboat, the pointed bow and flat stern. I hurry along the bank, slipping and falling as I go, but when I get close, I see that this rowboat is painted a deep green. It's not ours. I pull my fleece cap down tighter over my ears, and continue stumbling along the bank, hearing his voice in my mind, saying, "No bed more comfortable than the bottom of a boat a man built with his own hands," and, "The sky is the best kind of roof."

When I spot our boat, sobs leap into my throat. I scramble as fast as I can in the dry snow and crunchy soil toward the small handmade wooden craft. Its hull is completely iced in, the river frozen around it. A lump, wrapped in a snow-covered sleeping bag, lies motionless in the bottom of the rowboat, his head under one bench and his knees bent under the other. He's curled up on his side and definitely does not look comfortable.

"Dad!"

The lump doesn't move.

I hurl myself from shore to the boat, but stumble and fall. My face hits the edge of the gunwale and sharp pain radiates from my cheekbone. I gingerly touch the skin and my fingers come away dry. No blood. But the pain gives my resolve a razor's edge, and I climb into the boat next to the body. I pull back the sleeping bag and see Dad's shock of black hair.

I fit a hand under the bench and over his mouth. A whisper of warmth, breath. I reach under the sleeping bag and place my open palm on his chest. Yes, it's rising and falling. Dad might be the hardiest man on the planet. He can sleep outside the night of freeze-up, wrapped in only one sleeping bag, and survive.

I gasp for air, the shock of both cold and worry making breathing difficult as I get off my knees and sit on the stern-end bench of the boat. Shifting my weight causes the hull to crunch through the crust of ice. I squint out at the wide frozen river. The falling snow swirls and drifts across the mudflats. I look at my father, a man who hurt Keith, who burned my journal, who won't listen to anyone but his own inner voice, a voice that is becoming more impractical by the day. It's time for him to hear *my* voice.

I scoot forward and shake his shoulder hard. He moans. I shake him harder still, and he opens his eyes. Looks at me. Blinks a few times. He slides his head out from under the prow-end bench and sits up.

"Willa. I knew you'd change your mind. Where're your brothers?" Dad speaks quietly, but his rage pulses as bright as the Arctic light. It draws me, that rage, like magnetic north. The pull is so basic, so deep I feel a tingle in my feet, a kind of impulse pulling me back to him. To the rage, to the wilderness of everything I've lost.

I hoist myself back up onto the stern bench. We stare at each other.

Why haven't I seen it before? His rage is just sadness pushed to the point of explosion. He keeps pitting his strength against that sadness—dropping his family into the heart of a wilderness, building a cabin out of trees, hunting and butchering game, testing our ability to stay warm enough winter after winter, rowing solo down the Yukon River—as if one day he can conquer it.

It was Dad who taught me the difference between magnetic north and true north. Earth has fluid iron in its core. This molten iron exerts a strong magnetic pull, pointing to a place on the planet called magnetic north. This place moves, depending on that boiling iron core. Sometimes it's in the ocean. Sometimes it's on Greenland. True north, on the other hand, is where the lines of longitude meet in the Arctic. True north is a constant.

Dad's rage is magnetic north, and it draws me fiercely, confuses me, spins me until I'm dizzy. But there is a place inside me that is steely, unflinching. This is true north. It doesn't move. It knows—*I* know—what is true.

I stand up. The boat's hull crunches in the river's icy skin again. "No, Dad. I didn't change my mind. We're not going back to the cabin."

The rage blossoms in his eyes again. I think he might hit me. But instead of exploding, he implodes. His whole body slumps. He pulls the snowy sleeping bag up around his shoulders.

"How come *you* get to have friends?" I ask.

"Friends?"

"The ones you've been drinking with. Here in town."

"Those aren't friends."

His quick answer surprises me, gives me hope, and keeps me quiet for a few beats.

"You look exactly like Chloe," he says.

"What?" I whisper. Aunt Frances told me the same thing. I want to hear it over and over again.

Dad glares at the horizon. He's trying to muster his

anger. I need to reach him before it comes back to blind him.

"You listen to me now," I say.

He startles, like he's seen a ghost, and I suddenly remember that this is a phrase Mama used to use. I start talking and I don't stop for a very long time. I tell him about our whole journey, including the brown bear and the snow shelter and the ptarmigan meal and the hunters. I tell him that we didn't get on the plane this morning, even though I haven't a clue about how we're going to live this winter, but that Aunt Frances is here and she's going to help us figure it out. I even tell him about getting my period and how Amelia explained everything to me. The only part I don't tell him is how we hid in the riverside bushes and watched him row by. I keep that tender memory, the picture of him looking for us, tucked away for safekeeping.

I say, "You taught us how to find food and shelter in the meanest of circumstances. These lessons saved our lives."

He looks like he wants to speak, but I have to keep going or I might not be able to get out all I have to say. I hold up a hand to silence him.

"But there's more to survival than food and shelter," I say.

"You do. You look just like Chloe," Dad says again, his voice soft, as if he's seeing this, seeing *me*, for the very first time.

I'm so overwhelmed, I have to look away, into the snow flurries, and then I notice a dark splotch onshore, just a few feet from the boat. I realize it's *Jane Eyre*, which must have slid out of my parka pocket when I fell onto the rowboat. I climb over the gunwale and retrieve my book, holding it up so Dad can see.

"You didn't burn this," I say.

"That was your mother's favorite book."

"*This* book? This very copy?"

He nods.

I can no longer control my tears. "Why didn't you tell me this sooner?"

He just shakes his head. But I know why. He thinks that not talking about Mama will make the sadness go away. He's wrong. You can't run from it, not even if you go to extreme wilderness. Mama will always be with us, and even if it hurts, I'm glad. I want her memory with me. I slip *Jane Eyre* back into my pocket.

My voice is strong and clear as I tell him: "I want to go to school. I want friends. The boys need to be safe. We want more to eat than moose and mealy squash."

"Where are the boys?"

I ignore his question. "We took Zhòh up to a sanctuary for wolves. But a volunteer accidentally left a gate open. He got out. Seth is very upset."

"Who's Zhòh?"

"Zhòh is a wolf pup. Seth tamed him."

I want to tell Dad about the white wolf with glacier-blue eyes. How sanctuary wolves understand trauma, loss, and rediscovering the meaning of home and family. But right now I need to get him out of this boat, this snowstorm. He might be the hardiest man on the planet, but one day, like all of us, he'll meet his match. I'd like that to be later rather than sooner.

"Come with me," I say. "We're having breakfast in town."

He stands up and his legs wobble, but of course he won't let me help him out of the boat. Once onshore, he says, "I can find work for a week or two, make enough to pay for our chopper ride back to the cabin."

"We're not going back. Not the boys. And not me."

Dad doesn't answer. So I stand right in front of him. I can't stop him from drinking. I probably can't even stop him from making us all go back up to the cabin. But there's one thing I can do. I can speak my mind, my true north.

I reach up and take his two whiskery cheeks in my

hands. He flinches at my touch, but he doesn't move away. I wait until he meets my eyes.

"Did you hear me?" I say.

His eyes soften. His mouth trembles. He reaches out a hand and gently touches my cheek, the place where it hit the gunwale. Almost imperceptibly, he nods.

TWENTY-FIVE

WE BARELY ALL fit in the helicopter. Up front Hank the pilot checks his gauges and dials, getting ready for takeoff. Keith and Seth are squeezed in on either side of me and I'm holding their hands. I can feel Seth hyperventilating with excitement, his chest rising and falling. Keith is jiggling his left knee.

The chopper lifts straight off the Fort Yukon landing pad, like a bubble floating in the air, the blades whirling overhead. We rise into the sky, and Hank banks the helicopter so that the aircraft is nearly on its side.

In a matter of minutes, we'll be back where we started. We'll drift across the landscape in this giant motorized dragonfly, covering the same territory we hiked and rafted, a journey that took days and tested our courage. It can be undone this easily.

Hank rights the chopper again and we head north. From up here, Yukon Flats is a paisley of shapes, green islands tapering to points where the gray channels of the Yukon River swirl by. Soon Fort Yukon is gone, and even the Yukon River is behind us. I marvel at how small and inconsequential, even lazy and dreamy the rivers and streams appear from so far above. The mountains look cold and jagged, and the trees go on forever.

Keith spots our cabin first. He shouts, "There! I see it! Look!"

We all crane our necks to see out the windows, and Hank flies a wide circle in the sky so we can get a good look.

From above, our cabin seems vulnerable, just a small structure made of logs, its roof covered with moss and ferns. My garden is a tangle. The food cache stands off to the side on its spindly legs. The door to the outhouse hangs open, as if a bear has recently used the privy. Sweet Creek, just a trickle compared to the bigger rivers of Alaska, glistens along its course.

Eight months have passed since I found Dad sleeping in the rowboat. In that time the rivers froze solid, darkness descended for months, and blizzards raged across the tundra and through the mountains. Aunt Frances, the boys, and I spent the winter in Fort Yukon, living in a snug cabin belonging to Gwendolyn, a woman who sits on the Tribal Council with Stanley. She has a guest lectureship at the University of Oregon, and is super-happy to have us take care of her cabin while she's gone. Stanley says it's a win-win situation: we have a place to stay, and Gwendolyn's cabin is cared for.

Aunt Frances had to sublet her apartment in New York and take a leave of absence from her job to stay here and take care of us. She claims that she is moving back to New York just as soon as Dad gets out of rehab and is back on his feet. Constance winks at me, though, when Aunt Frances talks about how much she misses the city because by all appearances she's quite happy here. The people of Fort Yukon helped us so much in the beginning—bringing us casseroles and dry meat, as well as school clothes for me and the boys—that Aunt Frances wanted to give back to the community, so she started volunteering at the health clinic. When an administrative job opened up there, she got it. She likes to complain about how little it pays, compared to her job in New York, but she also likes to talk about how much cheaper it is living here, so it works out.

I loved every minute of school, even though I still

have a lot of catching up to do. Keith, on the other hand, struggled with the shock of so many new people and challenges. He picked fights with other boys and mouthed off at teachers. We don't know what we're going to do with him.

Seth is the big surprise. He still can't read very well, but he starred in the school's spring musical. He sang three solos. The audience gave him a standing ovation.

The very best part? Gwendolyn's cabin has two bedrooms. Aunt Frances gets one. Keith and Seth sleep in the main room. And...drumroll, please...I get the other bedroom. A whole room to myself with a door that shuts. Hank built me a bookshelf and now, alongside *Jane Eyre*, there are lots of other books.

Oh, and about *Jane Eyre*. Constance ordered Amelia her own copy from a bookstore in Fairbanks. Over the winter, during long evenings in front of the wood-burning stove, Amelia and I read it out loud together. She loves the story as much as I do.

Eventually, as spring arrived, the sun rose again. The days got longer and longer. The ice on the river thawed. And now summer has returned. The rivers run fat with snowmelt. The fireweed is shooting up in the meadows and soon their hot-pink buds will burst into bloom. The ptarmigans' feathers and the snowshoe hares' fur have turned from white to brown. The bears have emerged from their dens and are foraging for ground squirrels and roots. School is out, and June has arrived with its velvety-blue skies. Today is the solstice.

Visiting the cabin was my idea. I want to get it ready for Dad. All the adults tell me that Dad isn't my responsibility. They say I only have to look after myself now. Aunt Frances is in charge of the twins, and Dad has to make his own decisions. He hasn't been making great ones. He's in Fairbanks, enrolled in a treatment program. Everyone says that making that decision, agreeing to get treatment, is half the battle. I say he stopped drinking before, so he ought to be able to do it again. Still, his recovery hasn't been super-successful. He keeps falling off the wagon, which means he keeps drinking. The Johnsons have warned me: Sobriety is difficult. Lots of alcoholics never achieve it. That may be true, but I can still hope.

Meanwhile, I have a plan. The cabin is Dad's dream. It might be his true north, even if it isn't mine. I know he'll want to come back someday. Couldn't he stay here for a while? Without the bottles? He did it for so many years. Dad says that people are animals, and Stanley says that all animals circle back to home.

"Ready?" Hank asks from the cockpit. "Here we go."

Amelia, who is sitting up front with Hank, turns to

grin at me. I know she's grinning at the sound of Hank's voice. It always makes us laugh because it's so low and rumbly, like a motorcycle engine. Everything about him makes us laugh, especially his handlebar mustache. Just saying those two words, *handlebar mustache*, can get us hysterical.

Hank lands the helicopter gently on the hill above our cabin, in the exact spot where Dad shot his rifle straight up into the twilight and shouted at the sky. He shuts off the engine and we wait for the rotor blades to slow and stop. Keith insists on figuring out how to open the hatch himself, so that takes another couple of minutes, but soon we're all jumping out into the tall grasses. Aunt Frances, who rode in the farthest-back seat of the chopper, hurries away in a crouch position, even though the blades are no longer spinning, looking back as if the helicopter is an alien monster.

"Phew," she says. "That was terrifying."

"No way!" Keith, of course, disagrees. "I can't wait to go back up."

Seth starts running down the hill and I realize he's headed for Zhòh's old den. He knows perfectly well Zhòh will not be found in the den of his puppyhood. But that's Seth for you: Aunt Frances says he lives in a world of magical thinking.

As Amelia helps Hank take our lunch baskets out of the cages on the side of the helicopter, I turn and look at the cabin, down by the creek at the bottom of the hill. I can't believe I'm back. It's true that I'm here to ready the cabin for Dad, but it is also true that I need to see it for myself. This was the geography of my life for five years. We left so quickly. I never said goodbye.

"Oh, *boy*!" Amelia shouts. She leaves the lunch baskets with Aunt Frances and Hank and starts running down the hill. "Come on. Show me everything."

I follow slowly, taking big gulps of the tangy Arctic air, running my hands through the green grasses, and loving the bright mix of yellow buttercups, magenta shooting stars, and blue forget-me-nots. June is the month of vibrant, fecund growth in Alaska. The sun shines all day and night, the earth is saturated with the snowmelt, and all living things just go crazy. I remember how happy I've been every summer to see all the color, the blossoms of optimism.

At the bottom of the hill, I join Amelia, who's standing at the edge of my garden plot, hands on her hips, studying the profusion of growth. Without me here to tend it this spring, my garden is now just an overgrown riot of volunteers. Pumpkin vines sprawl every which way. Dark green kale leaves, oversized and bug-eaten, flap in the breeze. Amelia picks up a long, fat zucchini and swings it like a bat. "Strike one!"

Amelia can always make me laugh. I pick another zucchini and brandish it like a sword. Amelia grabs it from me and stuffs both squashes in her pack. Maybe we'll make zucchini bread when we get back to Fort Yukon.

Amelia hops up the porch steps and gestures at the door. "Open it!"

Opening that door feels like opening Pandora's box. I have no idea what memories will come flying out. I look around to see what everyone else is doing. Keith stands by the stream, tossing rocks into the water. He still won't let anyone cut his hair. He wears it tied back with a leather thong. Seth walks slowly down the hill toward his twin. I'm guessing that he's sad about having found Zhòh's den in a shambles. Winter would have collapsed whatever cozy nook the mama wolf built many months ago. Aunt Frances and Hank are standing on the hillside, watching.

I climb onto the porch and stop next to Amelia. She holds up her right pinkie and I link my right pinkie with hers. As we squeeze our fingers together, she grins her wide-open crazy grin, and our ritual gives me courage. I take hold of the wooden handle, worn smooth from five years of use, and pull the door open.

"Yowzer!" Amelia calls out, crowding in behind me.

A crusty bowl sits on the kitchen table, surrounded by rodent turds. Two mice skedaddle across the floor, diving into holes in the floorboards. I walk over to the woodstove and place my hand on top. Of course it's stone cold. Dad's Carhartt overalls and his blue-plaid-flannel shirt are wadded on his cot, as if he just recently scrambled out of his clothes. A whiskey-soaked stench permeates everything—the crumpled clothes, the canvas of the cots, even the wooden floor. My sneakers crunch on the broken glass covering the floorboards. I pick up the bottle's label, still stuck to a big shard of glass.

Holding the label, I imagine that day in October when Dad came home from hunting and found us gone. He must have been so angry. Or frustrated. Or maybe even heartbroken. I imagine him reaching up to open the high cupboard. The stale smell and whiskey-soaked cabin tell me that he probably didn't drink much. Instead he hurled the bottle with all his might. The explosion against the cast-iron woodstove, the whiskey splashing everywhere, the glass chiming as it shattered.

I take this as evidence that at least he *wants* to smash the bottles, that some part of him does want to stop drinking.

I shake out Dad's Carhartts and fold his shirt,

imagining how he must have put on his long underwear, fleece pants and sweater, the down parka, everything he'd need for the long journey. He took off after us as quickly as I'd expected he would. He chose *us* over that bottle. At least at first.

Amelia finds the homemade broom and begins sweeping up the mouse turds and glass. I pick up the foul soup bowl, carry it out the door and down to the creek. How familiar it feels to crouch at the water's edge with a dirty dish. I fill the bowl with water and set it on the pebbled beach to soak.

Aunt Frances is spreading out blankets in the meadow. Hank lopes down the hill—his legs are so long and skinny he looks like a moose when he walks— carrying the baskets of fried chicken, cornbread, straw- berries, and lamb's-quarters salad. The boys foraged for the lamb's-quarters, an edible wild leafy green, this morning, and Amelia made the dressing. Keith and Seth both run over to get a place on the lunch blanket. Keith reaches for the first piece of chicken.

As Amelia and I settle on the blanket, too, she leans toward me and whispers, "Handlebar mustache."

I glance at Hank and see that his mustache is full of cornbread crumbs.

We crack up.

"What?" Hank says in his deep motorcycle-engine voice. "Are you girls laughing at me again?"

He'll do anything to get us going. Walk on his hands. Hold the newspaper upside down and pretend he's reading it. Drink gravy with a straw. Now he starts threading wildflowers into his hair and making goofy faces at us.

Aunt Frances rolls her eyes and pretends that she's just tolerating Hank. But here's the truth. And it's a shocker. Ready?

Aunt Frances is *dating* the dude.

"In spite of myself," she likes to say, right in front of him.

"It's the Arctic air," Hanks replies. "Makes people do crazy things."

"Apparently," Aunt Frances agrees. "Whoever knew I could survive blizzards, wolves, and eternal darkness. That's all bad enough. But a six-foot-five-inch-tall mountain man? I must have gone clean off my rocker."

They go back and forth like this all the time, completely pleased with themselves. It's so embarrassing.

Sometimes I get upset when Aunt Frances talks about returning to New York. But Amelia says that all you have to do is watch how melty she gets around Hank. Constance agrees. "Frances isn't going anywhere," she assures me. "That man turns her inside out."

Whatever that means.

Last month I asked Aunt Frances point-blank if she was in love with Hank. She looked at me for a long time before answering. She didn't want to admit it. "Hank is the real deal," she finally said. "Genuine. You don't find that often."

Amelia and I think he's a big dork. But he sure is nice to us. And as long as Aunt Frances is all gaga, she might stay in Fort Yukon. We'll have to find another place to live when Gwendolyn returns from her guest lectureship at the University of Oregon, but Constance says finding a place to live in Fort Yukon is easy compared to finding one in New York.

Seth taps my knee and I think he wants me to pass him the container of chicken, so I do.

"No," he says in a whisper.

"The strawberries?" I ask.

"*Willa.*" The urgency in his whisper alarms me.

I start to gather him to me, thinking maybe he feels sick, or just needs a hug to help with the intensity of being back here at the cabin, but he wriggles out of my grasp and points. I follow his finger, which directs my gaze upstream.

I see Sweet Creek's sparkly water. The dark trees on either side. The slice of blue sky between the corridor of evergreen canopies. Beyond, the mountains in the golden solstice light. I turn back to Seth to ask what it is he wants me to see. But the look on his face silences me. He's staring so intently, as if his life depends on what he's seen, and so I look again.

This time I see something stir in the shadows beside the creek.

A moment later a large wolf steps into a patch of sunshine.

He's full-grown already, still a dark silver with white legs and a white mask. He's seen us and his black eyes go shiny, alert with recognition. He wags his tail, the white tip flicking back and forth. He stops twenty yards away and sits on his haunches.

Zhòh has circled back around to home.

Tears run down Seth's face. He whispers, "Come here, boy."

For a moment I think Zhòh's going to run right over to us, maybe leap into Seth's arms, but after standing and stretching the wolf seems to remember that he's wild now. He gives us one last long obsidian gaze before hoisting his tail as if to say, *See you later*. Zhòh turns and trots back upstream, into the heart of the wilderness.

ACKNOWLEDGMENTS

Thank you to my editor, Margaret Ferguson, and everyone at Holiday House; my agent, Reiko Davis; manuscript readers Pat Mullan, Elizabeth Stark, and children's librarian extraordinaire Armin Arethna; wolf expert Dorothy Hearst; and especially Sam Alexander, Gwichyaa Gwich'in from Fort Yukon.